The Redacte

C000151658

V

By

Orlando Pearson

Paperback ISBN 978-1-78705-579-7
ePub ISBN 978-1-78705-580-3
PDF ISBN 978-1-78705-581-0

Published by MX Publishing
335 Princess Park Manor, Royal Drive,
London, N11 3GX
www.mxpublishing.co.uk

Cover design Jane Dixon-Smith

For my family

Contents

A Perilous Engagement

It was the 14th of March 1907 when our client presented herself in the little sitting-room in Baker Street. My reader will have noted that many of the women whom Holmes and I encountered during our adventures were possessed of striking looks, spirit, and capabilities. The lady who stood before us was no exception to this. She was slight and short, but she radiated such youthful energy that it was impossible to imagine a dull moment in her company.

I think Holmes too was impressed. "And," he enquired solicitously, "are you the only woman in your Surrey shooting party?"

"Yes indeed, Mr Holmes," replied she in an assured voice. "My interest in field sports is unusual in my sex and so I am the party's only representative of the distaff side. I presume where I was early this morning before coming here, will have been betrayed to you by the Surrey loam on my shoes, and what I did there by the traces of powder on my shoulder which I have not yet had the opportunity to remove"

She gave my friend a searching look and then continued, "And, may I ask, has your violin, which I see in its case over there, been modified for playing by a left-handed player – I note that pugilism has left its mark in the form of swollen the knuckles on your left hand?"

My friend chuckled at our visitor's response. "I feel a foil as supple as my own," he replied. "To your point, my violin is a Stradivarius, so I would not venture to modify it in any way other than to tune it. But, when I put it to my chin, I play it as a right-handed person would. My preference, to which my biographer here has referred, for putting my violin on my lap and drawing the bow over the strings while it lies there, may be explained by my left-handedness."

Holmes paused before a look of solicitude came over his face. "And what brings you here straight from the field?" he asked

"I find shooting helpful when I want to release energy in moments of uncertainty. I have a most peculiar matter to relate. My name is Jean Leckie. I live in Kensington and I am of gentle stock. I am unmarried, but I have an unusual association with a member of parliament, Ignatius Foley, the member for Perth in Western Scotland."

"Mr Foley's name is of course known to me but not his association with you, dear lady. Perhaps you would elaborate."

"Mr Foley spends part of his time in London attending to parliamentary business and part of the time in his seat attending to his constituents' needs. His wife lives in Perth. She is consumptive, and her death is a matter of time. These taxing calls on his energies mean that he has no aspirations for political high-office, and he serves this country's democracy by being out-spoken on the back-benches. He had a highly successful legal practice before he went into politics and is an excellent public speaker. Ignatius and I have an understanding that we will marry once his wife is no more."

I certainly, and Holmes I think too, were taken aback by our client's candour in her description of her situation, but Holmes confined himself to the question, "And how may I be of assistance to you, madame?"

"I can see by the look on the faces of you two gentlemen that you find the relationship I have described a troubling one, but I can assure you that relations between Ignatius and me will remain of convential purity until such time as his present marriage comes to its natural end. Indeed, neither of us would have it any other way."

2

She paused, as though expecting an interjection from one of us, but we were both silent and she continued.

"Yesterday morning Ignatius came to our home. As usual I was chaperoned – on this occasion by my brother - and we sat in the lounge. Before Ignatius left, he reached into his jacket pocket to get out his diary so that we could arrange our next assignation – he is due to go up to his constituency tomorrow. He seemed to struggle to get his diary out and, when he did so, a heap of papers came up out of his pocket with it and scattered themselves over the floor. I made to help him pick them up, but he was, quite at variance to his normally imperturbable manner, extremely abrupt, and insisted on picking them up himself. He spent some time over this, and it was quite five minutes before he declared he had everything. My brother and I took Ignatius to the front door and he took his leave in very ill-humour. I returned to the lounge after Ignatius had gone and noted that he had failed to retrieve one document which was under the chaise longue."

"And what was the document?" Holmes enquired.

"It was a rental invoice for a property in London."

"What was so unusual about that? I imagine your fiancé must rent a flat for when he is in the capital on parliamentary duty."

"It was not made out to him."

She passed it to across to Holmes and me and I saw that it was addressed to a Mr James Turnavine for the rental of a flat at Denbigh Row in Fitzrovia.

"Mr Turnavine," she said, "is the Conservative member for Whitstable whereas Mr Foley is of the governing Liberal party. You are right to say," she continued, "that as a Scottish member of parliament, my fiancé needs a London residence, but his is at Charter Place in St. Giles, so the rental bill would have nothing to do with him. Instead, he has a bill relating to another member of parliament from a quite different part of the country, with a residence in a different part of London, and from a different party."

"As a man with a successful legal practice, your fiancé is a man of means," Holmes countered. "Could he have bought premises that he has rented out to another member of parliament?"

"That was, Mr Holmes, of course, the first explanation that came to my mind although my fiancé has never mentioned owning any property in London. But the invoice is from Fitzrovia Estates and my research yesterday afternoon showed this is a company belonging to the Duke of Grafton who owns all the properties in the Fitzrovia area; so my fiancé cannot be a landlord at Denbigh Row."

"You seem to have a remarkable talent for investigative research. What are your next steps to be?"

"Well, I really came here to hear a theory from you rather than to propose a course of action," said our visitor.

There was a long pause while Holmes considered the matter. He rose to check his files before he sat down again.

"I have commented," he said at length, "in another case that men do not normally carry the bills of other men around in their pockets. They have quite enough of their own to settle. Then the bill was a clue in a case of a corrupt horse trainer who was leading a double life with a false identity, but my files confirm the separate identity of Mr Turnavine from Mr Foley."

Holmes paused again.

"In the absence of any more material, I think the best thing I can do is to summarise the very limited facts before us. Your betrothed had with him a pile of documents which he was very anxious to retrieve when they fell out of his pocket. Nevertheless, he failed to retrieve one which is a rental invoice made out to another man, and you are unable to find an explanation for this, although you fear it may be discreditable to your fiancé."

"That is so."

"Has your fiancé noticed the missing document and made any attempt to retrieve it?"

"He has not but he will have been on an overnight train to Perth last night, so I would not have expected him to do so even if he was aware that he had failed to pick up one document."

"Then, dear madame, I would suggest you return home. I will contemplate your disquisition and revert to you if any insight occurs to me. I would suggest that you yourself give some thought to the background of the matters you have raised with me. Consider whether there has been any other occasion when your betrothed might have displayed agitation and why that might have been so. Cast your mind back to try to recall whether he has ever mentioned any interests in properties? Any further particulars would be of the greatest interest to me in what appears to me to be a most peculiar matter."

Miss Leckie's footsteps were still audible on the staircase when there was the sound of two sets of feet coming up. The street door below banged loudly shut as the buttons opened the door to our sitting room to announce the arrival of Mycroft Holmes.

As my reader may recall, after the adventure of *The Bruce Partington Plans* of late 1895 Mycroft Holmes makes no further appearances in the stories I have chosen should appear in my lifetime. This was due to a falling out between my friend and his brother after the events described therein. This second matter is related in the story *The Sleeper's Cache*. In spite of my embargo on the publication of further stories featuring Mycroft Holmes, my friend continued to help his brother on political matters after the fissure in their relationship but, as my reader will see, the nature of the events I now describe would in any case have rendered this story unpublishable for at least one hundred years after the time they occurred

As he sat down, Mycroft (to whom I shall refer as Mycroft while I refer to Sherlock Holmes as Holmes) displayed an agitation which I might refer to as quite theatrical. His bulky frame twitched with tension and his gaze flitted in all directions as he twice took pinches of snuff before he started speaking.

"Sherlock," he said, "I would that you go to the continent immediately. I will travel with you to Victoria Station, and we will wait under the clock there to meet a man from the Bulgarian secret police. There is a matter for you to resolve which affects the entire power balance of Europe. You will need to travel with him to Sofia and there is an express to Dover at noon. You will be in the Bulgarian capital by tomorrow evening." Mycroft turned to me. "I fear, dear doctor, that the Bulgarians were insistent that only my brother should come and help them."

My friend sat in thought for some time, mindful that some of the other commissions he had received from his brother were more freighted with political implications than had met the eye.

Nevertheless, after a few minutes he rose, packed his bag with a few small items, and left with Mycroft.

I sat thinking for an hour about the case that our fair visitor of that morn had brought us.

Had I ever had a rental bill to another man in my pocket and, once I had established in my mind that I had not, what possible reason might there have been for me to have one?

I was about to ring the bell for lunch when here was a hesitant knock on the door.

"Come!" I said, and Miss Leckie stood once again at the threshold of the sitting room.

"Is Mr Holmes not here?" she asked.

"I fear he has been called away on urgent business. I cannot tell you when he will return."

"I feared that might be so," said she. "In that case, Dr Watson, could I ask you to look at my petition anew for I have found some more material. Would you have time to do so before you go out?"

I had formed no plan to leave the flat at Baker Street but let the matter pass in my eagerness to assist the young petitioner.

"I am happy to do so, madame", I said, "but I would advise you that my previous efforts at detective work have had results that have been mixed at best."

"I need someone whom I can trust to talk to," said she with a smile that would have won over a stonier heart than mine.

She passed to me a scrap of paper.

"When I got home, the living room felt cold and I decided to add some coals to the fire. I found this in the coal scuttle which is next to where Mr Foley sat when he was with me yesterday."

I looked at the paper which still bore signs of having been in contact with coal dust. It was another accounting document - this time a bill from the Bar of Gold in Upper Swandham Lane in London's docklands. The only entry on it said 'Two pipes at four shillings'. There was no indication of whether the bill was made out to Mr Foley, but the Bar of Gold's name was at the top.

"Madame," I said gravely, "I fear that I could not put any sort of construction on the rental bill you said came from your fiancé, but which was addressed to another member of parliament. This document, by contrast, is from an establishment in a most notorious part of London, and I fear you will find the explanation for it only discreditable."

"You say so, Dr Watson, and that was my immediate reaction too, yet your conclusion leaves so much unclarified."

"Perhaps you would like to expand on your thesis."

"If, as you surmise, the Bar of Gold is a dubious establishment, why would it issue a receipt and why would anyone wish to keep it? And look at the date on the bill. It is from the 25th of January of last year."

I still had the bill in my hand and when I glanced again at it, I noted the accuracy of Miss Leckie's remark.

"Why," she continued, "would my fiancé have it in his pocket a year after it was issued? I would also advise you that while my fiancé enjoys a cigarette or a pipe like any normal man, and is the father of two children, he has never in our acquaintance displayed the least interest in the sorts of titillations you imply might be on offer at the Bar of Gold."

In retrospect, on the facts, I may have been somewhat generous in what I said next.

"Very well Madame, I will go down to the Bar of Gold and form a view of what sort of establishment it is."

"If the Bar of Gold is a lubricious establishment, is that not a somewhat perilous engagement?"

"Madame," I replied, "I feel that you are the one with the perilous engagement and that you deserve clarity on the motives of your betrothed."

"But I must come with you. I have…" she glanced at her watch.

"We are, madame," I interjected, "already in breach of propriety in that you and I are alone in a room together unattended by anyone of an equivalent social class. This is only permissible because you yourself have entered the room unannounced and I had no idea who it was when you knocked. But I cannot sit in a carriage with you without a third person of suitable social standing being present, and I do not wish to wait for a third person to make themselves available. I shall undertake this part of the investigation myself. Do you have a photograph of Mr Foley?"

"I have it here."

"I would that all of Mr Holmes's clients were so skilled at anticipating his needs, dear lady."

In a minute I was on the pavement at Baker Street and had hailed a hansom. I was about to step into it when I discovered that I only had one cigarette left in my case. I went to the tobacconist on the corner of Baker Street and Marylebone Road to replenish my supplies before hailing another cab. A drive of three quarters of an hour found me in Upper Swandham Lane.

Some of my readers will already know of the Bar of Gold. I say this, not because I would wish to cast aspersions on any of them, but because the establishment formed a key part in the events related in *The Man with the Twisted Lip* which took place in June 1889. I had visited it to try to rescue my patient, the sottish opium addict, Isa Whitney, from it and commented then that it was the vilest opium den in London.

I felt that nothing was likely to have changed but was determined, armed with the photograph of Mr Foley, that I should at least try to establish whether the member of parliament for Perth had been inside.

I confess that I was not at all sure of the wisdom of this course of action and it was with foreboding that I mounted the stairs worn hollow in the centre by the ceaseless tread of addled feet. I made my way into a long, low room, thick and heavy with the brown opium smoke. Through the gloom I could dimly catch a glimpse of bodies lying in strange poses, bowed shoulders, bent knees, heads thrown back, and chins pointing upward, with here and there a dark, lack-lustre eye turned upon the newcomer. Out of the black shadows, there glimmered little red circles of light, now bright, now faint, as the burning poison waxed or waned in the bowls of the metal pipes.

A sallow Malay attendant hurried up with a pipe for me and a supply of the drug, beckoning me to an empty berth.

I took it with some misgivings, struck a match, and took the smallest possible pull on the pipe. To my surprise the Malay pinned a slip of paper to my berth and marked it.

"Is that something you always do?" I asked.

"Sir, you are obviously new to this. Of-course we keep a check on what each berth has consumed. I'll collect the money from you when you leave. Letting you pay at the end helps you to forget, while marking down your consumption helps us to remember."

He left me, and I rose to look at the chit.

I expected to see a headed document like that which Miss Leckie had found left behind by Mr Foley but instead I found just a slip of blank paper with a single tick on it. Having got myself into the Bar of Gold, I now wondered through the cloying haze of burning pipes how I might prosecute my investigation.

And then I had a stroke of good fortune. There was an altercation at the entrance, and on striding to the front of the establishment to see what was afoot, I found myself face to face with my former patient, Mr Isa Whitney, in a furious argument with the Lascar manager of the Bar of Gold.

"Watson, how good to see a friend," wheezed Whitney through the haze. "I fear there has been a complete misunderstanding with the good proprietor of this establishment. I think it would be as well if I departed."

"Whitney!" I exclaimed, "How long have you been here for?"

"We don't use names in here," interjected the Lascar. "Ever."

"A couple of hours, maybe three," mumbled Mr Whitney.

"Then why do you have the *Evening Standard* from three days ago in your pocket?"

"What day is it?"

"It is Thursday afternoon."

"Surely it is only Monday. I have had perhaps three pipes, maybe four. Not more."

"It is Thursday," I replied firmly. "I will take you home. Your wife will be out of her mind with worry. How much does Mr Whitney owe you?" I asked the Lascar.

"Fourteen shillings and fourpence halfpenny – and I said we don't use names in here," snapped the Lascar. "But it won't be the first time this man has made difficulties." I was about to ask whether I might have a receipt when the proprietor roared, "Now get ye both gone before it be the worse for ye."

I settled the amount outstanding, went out onto the street, and was able to summon a cab when an idea dawned on me. I may not be able to make an extended observation of the interior of the Bar of Gold but, if Mr Whitney was still a habitué of the establishment, I could ask him whether he recognised the photograph of Mr Foley.

On the way back to Mr Whitney's house near Paddington my former patient's mood swung violently between clarity and hysteria but in one of his lucid moments I showed him the photograph of Foley.

He stared at it for some time. "Well, we get all sorts in there – tars and tarts, quacks and queers, pawnbrokers and pornographers, politicians, lawyers, and journalists – but I don't remember him." That was as much as I could get out of him and I had soon left him back at his home and returned to Baker Street.

"The lady is back for you again," said the buttons, when I arrived. "I didn't want her to go up, but she insisted on waiting for you in the upstairs flat."

"I am so sorry to have come back for a third time today," said my petitioner, when I entered the sitting room, "but I have made a further discovery that I would share with you."

"I have got nowhere in establishing whether your betrothed was in the Bar of Gold," I countered gloomily.

"Nor have I – or to be more precise – I have found evidence that he was not, but that only makes the matter more mysterious."

"Please explain."

"I keep a careful record both of my movements of those of my betrothed as we need to ensure that we can see each other as often as possible while allowing hm to attend to his constituency duties and to his wife's needs. I checked my diary for last year and found that on the evening of the 24th of January 1906, my brother and I accompanied Ignatius to Euston Station whence he boarded the night train to Perth."

"Could he not have alighted at an intermediate stop and returned to London."

"My local library gets copies of both national and local newspapers and I was able to find the *Perth Weekly Informer* of the 26th of January of last year. It states: 'Mr Foley gave a brief speech as he opened the new orphanage at Fraser Terrace at eleven o'clock in the morning of the 25th of January,' and in a separate article it says, 'The Perth Society of Whisky Producers held its annual Burns Night supper yesterday evening. After the piping in of the haggis, the members were addressed by Perth's member of parliament, Mr Ignatius Foley'. My betrothed was thus indubitably four hundred or more miles from the Bar of Gold on the 25th of January of last year."

"I must commend you on both the thoroughness of your investigation and on its speed but, I concur with you, that this only makes matters only more mysterious. You have excluded the possibility of your fiancé from having been in the Bar of Gold on the date for which you have the bill, but can think of no reason, disreputable or otherwise, why he should be carrying this receipt on his person when he was not actually there."

"Dr Watson, my discussions with you have hardened my resolve. I cannot live with the uncertainty the discovery of these documents is causing me. Mr Foley is back in London next Tuesday and I will confront him with my findings. My brother is away at present, and I would like you to act as my chaperone."

Miss Leckie looked me directly in the eye and I confess it was hard to deny her this request.

"Very well," I said, "I think you are well advised to clarify the matter with him. Who will you say that I am?"

"I have an uncle Horace of whom Ignatius has heard tell but has ever met. I will introduce you as him."

So it was that a few days later I found myself at the Leckie house in Kensington when the maid brought in Mr Ignatius Foley. He was a tall man with a bluff manner. He expressed no surprise at my presence, and he and Miss Leckie sat down before the fire while the maid brought them tea.

After initial pleasantries, in which Miss Leckie displayed a degree of froideur towards her beau which seemed to pass him by, Mr Foley made the first conversational gambit.

"And Miss Jean, how would you like at, some point in the future, to be Lady Foley. For I am to be made attorney general quite soon. The post carries with it not only a princely salary but a knighthood."

"Why this sudden political advancement?" asked Miss Leckie, I think somewhat repelled by the politician's self-congratulatory air. "A man with a constituency in a distant part of the country, a sick wife, and a pining fiancée, is not likely to be in a position to take on the additional responsibilities of high office. And I am not aware of anything you have done to catch the eye of the prime minister and so persuade him to promote you to this lofty position."

"Events, dear Jean, events," Foley breezed. "Some are beyond our control. Some we can influence. They have unexpected consequences for us all – some for good, some for ill. Life's winners turn events into opportunities. The prime minister was most insistent I should take the post, and I would be most reluctant to disoblige him."

15

"What events?" pressed Miss Leckie, but he would not be drawn further.

There was a pause and then Miss Leckie countered.

"Ignatius, I have a matter of great concern which I would like to raise with you. When you were here last week you dropped some papers from your pocket. You displayed great agitation about these papers and insisted vehemently that you and you alone should pick them up."

"I recall an incident when I dropped some documents of a purely administrative nature but not any untoward agitation to retrieve them."

He paused, but I thought he would continue. Several seconds elapsed before I realized he was waiting for Miss Leckie to speak.

"You were, if I may say so, dear Ignatius," she eventually ventured, "abrupt in the extreme when my brother and I sought to help you to pick up the papers."

"Well, what of it?"

"In spite of your agitation to pick up the papers, I subsequently found two that you had failed to observe. One was for an opium den called the Bar of Gold, and the other was a rental bill for a fellow member of parliament. I can think of no reason that is not discreditable for the first item to be in your pocket. I have no explanation at all for the second."

Foley went white as the spirited Miss Leckie spoke although he soon recovered his composure.

"I can give you my word that I have never been to any opium den," he replied at last.

"I can, you may be surprised to know," countered she, "regard that as possible since I was able to establish that you were not in London on the day the bill was raised. But that does not of course explain its presence in your pocket."

He was silent.

"And why did you have the rental bill of another member of parliament in your pocket? Under the chaise longue you left a bill for a month's rent for a member from another party?"

"Really? Which one?"

"It is of no moment which member or which party. I can think of no satisfactory explanation for either document being on your person."

"You may," he responded, cautiously and not entirely convincingly, "have misunderstood the nature of politics. In politics, one's enemies are in one's own party as members of parliament from one's own party are the people with whom I am in competition for ministerial preference. Members of other parties, by contrast, do not constitute a barrier in the way of one's political advancement, and are opponents with whom one occasionally works to get things done. I am accordingly in regular though not frequent discussion with members of other parties."

"That hardly explains why you would have a document personal to another member of parliament. Does this flirtation with a member of another political party have anything to do with your political advancement?"

"How could dealings with a member of another party enable me to win the favour of the prime minister?"

"It is I who must ask the questions. I am the person who is sacrificing her youth in the hope that we can get married when you are free. You have a wife and children. You have already had a life with another. I am hoping to have one with you and have foresworn all others to do so. It is I who is risking her future happiness for, while I can be confident that I could find a suitable match if our betrothal should come to an end now, my confidence of this diminishes with every day that passes."

Foley was silent and eventually it was Miss Leckie who spoke again.

"I repeat, have these documents to do with your sudden political advancement?"

"Dear Jean, there are matters of state the workings of which you cannot possibly understand and which I cannot divulge to you. As politicians we have a duty to our individual constituents, to the population at large, and to the state. These duties will sometimes conflict so one will undertake actions on behalf of an individual to protect him from the state, or on behalf of the state to preserve its reputation. I fear I cannot give you a more detailed answer than that although I would assure you that I have done nothing that is dishonourable towards you, towards my party, or towards my country – indeed, if my actions are to be judged at all, they may be said to have served to protect the reputation of this country and all that it stands for."

"But that is no answer to my concerns. Is there no further information you can give me?"

"I would refer you to my previous responses to your questions."

"Mr Foley, I had hoped you would have an answer that would put my concerns to rest but you have not. I will need to consider whether you are worthy of my affections. Our relations are of far more moment to me than a mere flirtation between a man who is old enough to know better and a young girl who is not. I will write to you if decide I wish to see you again. Uncle Horace, would you escort Mr Foley to the door."

After Mr Foley left, I felt that I had little to say to Miss Leckie. I would not wish her to see my admiration for her stand against her fiancé in case she felt that I had a motive behind it. I left her, and, feeling the need for a change of scene, spent the evening at my club.

I rose late the following day, and on descending to the sitting room, found breakfast already laid out on the table. I lifted the cloche on one dish and was about to start to eat when Holmes entered.

"I normally," he started as he sat down, "feel uncomfortable without my biographer at my side but you missed nothing in not joining me. The case I was asked to investigate had nothing of complexity – indeed, contrary to what Mycroft had told me – the local police were already well on the way to clearing up the conspiracy against the Bulgarian leader. I telegraphed Mycroft from the telegraph office at Victoria on my arrival and he will be here shortly for a full debrief. And, how have you filled the last few days?"

I gave my friend an account of the developments in the case that had first been brought to our attention by Miss Leckie. As I expatiated on them, Holmes sat upright in his chair. Eventually he said, "Well, this matter strikes me as being of considerably greater moment than what Mycroft asked me to investigate."

"Really?" I countered. "I appreciate Miss Leckie has a personal dilemma, but I hardly think that what appears to me to be a personal matter compares to a matter of state like the one to which you have referred."

"Good Watson, while I must commend you on your courage in venturing into the Bar of Gold, and congratulate Miss Leckie on the speed and thoroughness of her investigative techniques, I fear that both of you have missed the solution to a case that is at the same time trivial in its substance, grave in the way it would be perceived by the public, and of great consequence to her personally. I fear that clarifying the case for Miss Leckie without placing both her and the stability of the state in peril is something that is beyond even my powers."

"Perhaps you could explain."

"I will start with the resolution of the case which is facile in the extreme although I will have to conduct one brief interview to confirm my opinion."

"So, what were these documents?"

"It is clear that neither of the documents Miss Leckie retrieved were personal to Mr Foley. It is also clear - and here is a point both you and Miss Leckie have missed in your investigation - that he had no idea of precisely what documents he was carrying as he attached great importance to their recovery when he dropped them but failed to realise subsequently that he had been unsuccessful in retrieving them all."

"But you still have not explained what these documents were," I insisted.

"Mr Foley was under interrogation by his betrothed when he said that the documents were of a purely administrative nature and that they had not been addressed to him. These two facts make it likely that he was telling the truth on both points, and this theory is borne out by the two documents that Miss Leckie found."

"So why was he carrying a sheaf of administrative documents that belonged to other people?"

"An intellectual scintillation is required by you here, good Watson. Where might you find administrative documents in large numbers belonging to several or many different people?"

"I would say at the post office, but I hardly think that Mr Foley would be abstracting documents from a post office."

"Not in a post office, dear Watson, but in an accounts office. Mr Foley has broken into an accounts office and scooped up as many accounting documents as he could lay his hands upon."

"Can you prove which accounts office?"

"Mr Mycroft Holmes to see you, Mr Holmes," the voice of our buttons interrupted before Holmes could answer my question.

"It is good to see you return from your eastern Europe sojourn, dear brother," said Mycroft as he entered. "I have another

21

commission for you which will also require your absence from London."

"Good day to you, brother Mycroft," said Sherlock Holmes. "I have remarked to my friend Watson here, that you often *are* the British government – the great clearing house of all its thinking on diverse matters such as the bimetallic question and India. I suspect you are about to demonstrate this for us now on an entirely separate matter."

"Pray be brief then, good brother, in the exposition of your problem," replied Mycroft. "It is most crucial that you undertake this second overseas mission and most undesirable that I be away from Westminster for any length of time. It gives the prime minister and his acolytes the wholly erroneous impression that they can run the country on their own."

"Very well," replied my friend. "Why then, may I ask, as a good citizen of this country, have you not called the police in to investigate the recent burglary of the accounts office of the Houses of Parliament or the Serjeant-at-Arms' Office, as it is normally called?"

Mycroft started violently. "How do you know about that? I have taken the most extreme measures to make sure that that does not get into the press just yet. I would even go so far as to say that your fruitless mission to Bulgaria was not unconnected with the break in."

"Perhaps you would like to expand on your remark."

"Parliament has been rocked with rumours that members have been submitting inappropriate expense claims. If proof of this was brought to the attention of the public, there would be general outrage and the role of our parliamentary representatives, aye even of parliament itself, would be called into question."

"Pray continue."

"Just over two weeks ago, an intruder was apprehended by one of our night security staff. The trespasser was just leaving the office of the Serjeant-at-Arms where the expense records of members of parliament are kept. After a struggle, the intruder was apprehended, and a capacious briefcase prised from his grasp. When the matter was reported to me, I had the intruder brought before me and made sure I was the only person present when I forced the case open."

There was a pause and Mycroft took a large pinch of snuff.

"When I did so I found it contained all the expense claims for the last two years from members of parliament whose surnames ran from N to T. And the claims were for some of the most outlandish things. Alongside claims for things one would expect such as overnight accommodation and travel, one member had claimed to have turrets added to his house, and another had claimed on an invoice from an establishment the nature of which I could not possibly disclose even to you, good brother."

"And to whom did you report the burglary if not the police?"

"The intruder is a member of parliament from the governing party so naturally I reported the matter to the prime minister."

"And what was his reaction?"

"As I had anticipated, the burglary was at the prime minister's behest. He was horrified that the break-in's objective had been thwarted. Like me, he felt that it was best that the matter obtained the smallest possible coverage. There will be a cabinet reshuffle shortly. The intruder will be appointed to a ministerial post in which he will be in a position to ensure that should any information on the matter gain currency, nothing substantive will be done to investigate it."

"And what other steps did you take?"

"I went down to the office of the Serjeant-at-Arms and made sure all the filing cabinets with members' expense claims were completely emptied and their contents burnt. We cannot have the reputation of the mother of parliaments sullied by the egregious behaviour of its members getting into the press."

"So, what will you do next?"

"In a few days' time, I shall ensure that a discrete mention is made of the burglary in some minor organ of the press."

"Why will you do that?"

"Well, obviously, if the main body of the national newspapers should subsequently get hold of the much bigger story of fraudulent expense claims by members of parliament, I can then tell them that all documentary evidence of expense claims has been destroyed and refer them to the burglary, an account of which will already have been published. Their embarrassment at having failed to notice this story will be quite sufficient to dissuade them from pursuing the matter of the expenses of members of parliament any further - particularly as there will be nothing material to show what has happened and why. Thus, all will be well."

"And did you get all the incriminating evidence of inappropriate claims?"

"The minutiae of investigation are more an area for your expertise than for mine. When I debriefed him, the prime minister asked me if I had searched the intruder's person, which I had not. It is therefore possible that the intruder had further documents on his person which we failed to retrieve but, as his objective was to destroy evidence of wrongdoing, he will doubtless have taken steps to give effect to that in any case."

"And I assume you have rewarded the member of security staff who apprehended the intruder. To take on and apprehend an intruder single-handed at night would have taken significant courage."

"On the contrary, good brother, an entirely separate investigation into the timekeeping of our security staff has revealed some regrettable lapses of accuracy in recording for both for the apprehender of the intruder and some of his colleagues. They have all been advised that no action will be taken at this juncture but that the matter can be re-opened at any time should their behaviour prove in any other way to be unsatisfactory."

Mycroft evidently considered the matter of the burglary closed and there was a brief pause before he said.

"And now for the matter at hand. This will take you to some of our most far-flung colonies – probably for several months. And I can assure you that there may be a knighthood at the end of it if the task is carried out to my satisfaction."

"Dear brother, that I cannot treat with someone who suppresses news of wrong-doing in the mother of parliaments."

"Are you saying, Sherlock, that you will not act on this commission that I would wish you to fulfil in spite of the signal honour that will be bestowed on you following its satisfactory completion?"

"I fear that I cannot allow myself to be manoeuvred out of the country to help you out of a political embarrassment."

There was a long pause.

"In that case, dear brother, I would advise you and Dr Watson to keep this matter to yourselves. Any public reference to it will have unfortunate consequences for you and anyone else with whom you communicate on it."

Mycroft was soon on his way and Holmes leaned back in his chair.

"You see Watson, I had no idea at all that a burglary had taken place in the office of the Serjeant-at-Arms, but no other explanation fitted the facts. Only an accounts office would hold personal invoices from a number of different people, and only one located in the Houses of Parliament would hold invoices from politicians. And only a burglary would explain how Mr Foley could have been in possession of such personal documents which clearly did not relate to him and the only value of the documents was that the bearer of them could claim expenses on them. And only an attempt to cover up a scandal would explain why no news of the break-in had leaked out."

"And you do not want to investigate this matter further?"

"I fear that I can see no good coming out of an investigation – indeed only harm."

"And why would an establishment such as the Bar of Gold issue a receipt to someone who patronised it? I got no document of any sort when I paid Mr Whitney's bill?"

"Because the member of parliament who frequented it asked for one – a rather obvious investigative step the omission of which by you I previously forbore to point out."

"Why would whatever member of parliament it was who visited the Bar of Gold ask for an invoice?"

"Well, obviously, so that he could claim it on his expenses. Being a member of parliament is very far from being an occupation that fills all of one's time, so our representatives seek diversions to combat their ennui for which they then seek to get recompensed. But they can only be recompensed if they have a bill or a receipt against which to claim."

"And what do you want me to tell Miss Leckie about her fiancé?"

Having answered my questions until now with an almost dismissive fluency, my colleague paused at this latest one and knocked the ash from his pipe into the grate before responding.

"I cannot give her and her alone information that will undermine the foundations of the country and the possession of which will put her into grave peril. You saw how eager Mycroft is to prevent the matter becoming public knowledge, and I cannot exclude him taking the most extreme measures to protect his secret. Accordingly, you will have to tell her that her discoveries are a matter of state that I cannot divulge. You should not present my refusal to disclose anything more as an endorsement of the conduct of her betrothed. You may also wish to commend her for her investigative ability which is of a calibre far in advance of that displayed by the professionals at Scotland Yard."

"It will be I who has to tell her?" I asked, somewhat nettled that this task should have been delegated to me. "How do you think she will react to that?"

"Yes, how do you think I will react?" came a voice from under the breakfast table.

Miss Leckie emerged from beneath the table-cloth and stood before us looking quite undiscommoded by her period of concealment.

"I had worked out that my fiancé's action had serious political consequences, Mr Holmes. I know the role of your brother in government. And, when I saw a man who from the shape of his skull was obviously your brother, mounting the stairs as I left here two weeks ago, that confirmed it. I banged the street door closed but concealed myself in the hallway till the buttons had gone back to his domestic duties, and then crept back up the stairs. I listened outside your door to your brother's petition and realised that I would not get an answer to my own petition until you were back in the country."

I glanced at Holmes during Miss Leckie's account of her actions and was amused to note a look of wonder on his face at Miss Leckie's detective skills.

She continued. "Accordingly, I met each boat train as it arrived at Victoria Station and watched for your return. When I saw you descend from the train this morning, I sprang into a hansom, and beat you back to Baker Street. On my arrival here, I was asked to wait downstairs as you were not in and Dr Watson had not risen from his slumbers. When breakfast was laid out for Dr Watson, it was an obvious step to conceal myself in the sitting room."

"You are a remarkable woman," said Holmes thoughtfully. "You have investigative zeal, insight, and resourcefulness. I fear however for your well-being as you have been a witness to the state-sponsored suppression of a great scandal."

There was a long pause before Holmes spoke again.

"Although he did not divulge it to us, Mycroft knows exactly who stole the accounting documents at the Serjeant-at-arms office, and although I know that you have exercised discretion in your conduct with Mr Foley, my brother will have the resources to track down your fiancé's antecedents. He is almost bound to want to investigate how I got to know about this matter."

"Are you suggesting that I need some form of protection?" asked Miss Leckie. "I am sure I am capable of looking after myself."

"I have no doubt that you are more than equal to combatting most threats, but here all the forces of the state may be arraigned against you. I do indeed believe you will need someone of courage and dedication to protect you."

"I should myself be most happy to help," I heard myself saying, as I realised the happy conjunction of Miss Leckie's need and my own feelings towards her.

"Good Dr Watson," said the fair Miss Leckie, and I thrill to this day at the memory of the dazzling smile she gave me as she said it, "I greatly admire both the correctness in your behaviour towards me and your lion-hearted courage in entering the Bar of Gold in pursuit of the prosecution of my case. I can think of no one who I would rather have as to protect me from peril than you."

A smile ghosted over the face of Sherlock Holmes. "Very well," said he, "then what Sherlock Holmes has brought together, let no man sunder."

Death at Tennis

The matter that follows exposes shocking behaviour in a royal family which, although not the British house, will be one well-known to my reader. It also chronicles the closest that Holmes and I came to a permanent rift in our friendship for reasons which have more to do with what I continue to regard as a rare lapse in Holmes's judgment than to any deliberate slight to me on his part. In the end, however, I formed the view that the benefits of our friendship outweighed the very real hazards to me from our association. There will be others who take a different view – whether to perceive Holmes's behaviour as justified, or to think that a termination of our friendship justified. I have set out the debate we had at the resolution of one part of the case as it happened and will leave it to my readers to make their own judgment.

After my second marriage in the autumn of 1907, I saw little of Holmes. My own complete happiness, and the home-centred interests which rise up around the man who is once more master of his own establishment, absorbed all my attention. For his part, Holmes, who loathed every form of society with his whole Bohemian soul, had remained in our lodgings in Baker Street.

I returned to civil practice. One night, as I was returning from a journey to a patient, my way led me through Baker Street. As I passed the well-remembered door, forever associated in my mind with my first wooing, I was seized with a keen desire to see Holmes again. His rooms were brilliantly lit, and, even as I looked up, I saw his tall, spare figure pass twice in silhouette against the blind. I rang the bell and was shown up to the chamber which had once been in part my own. His manner was not effusive. It seldom was; but he was glad, I think, to see me. With hardly a word spoken, but with a kindly eye, he waved me to an armchair, threw across his case of cigars, and indicated a spirit case and a gasogene in the corner.

"It is fitting indeed," he remarked at last, "that your visit here following on hard after your wedding should coincide with my next consultation."

"What is so fitting about it?" I asked.

"My next client is Wilhelm Gottsreich Sigismund von Ornstein, Grand Duke of Cassel-Feldstein, and hereditary King of Bohemia, or Count Gustav von Kramm, which was the name he gave himself when we first met."

"The former lover of Irene Adler, and whose case I chronicled under the title *A Scandal in Bohemia* as the first case we investigated after the start of my first marriage?"

"The same."

"What does he want to see you about?"

"His missive did not specify but I hear his feet on the stairs so we will soon find out."

The King entered.

The intervening nineteen years had not been kind to him. He had been rendered breathless by climbing the seventeen steps from the street to the flat, and his great height had been diminished by a stoop. All that was left of his hair was plastered in grey streaks across his pate. In contrast to his hollowed-out physique, the outfit he had chosen – with heavy bands of astrakhan slashed across the sleeves and fronts of his double-breasted coat – gave him an air of unreality. It was as if he were a character from a fairy story. It was a while before he could summon enough breath to address us at all.

"Mr Holmes," he said at last in his deep harsh voice with its strongly marked German accent, "I sent you a message that I would call, and, as at my visit in '88, I see Dr Watson here as well. I hope this coincidence is a portent for a solution to my problem as happy as that of two decades ago."

"My recollection of that case, Your Majesty, is that I was completely outwitted by your former mistress, Miss Irene Adler," replied Holmes drily. "She saw through my disguise as a Congregationalist parson, and she realised why I was pursuing her. She then disguised herself as a man and followed me back here. I failed to see through her disguise even when she had the temerity to wish me a good night. And by the next morning she had vanished abroad taking with her the photograph of you and her that I had been seeking to recover on your behalf."

There was a pause and the King seemed to be in a trance at the mere thought of the behaviour of Miss Adler. He then came to and gave a dismissive wave.

"Your actions dissuaded my former paramour from sending a compromising photograph to my then betrothed, and so saved the honour of my royal house. That was to me an entirely satisfactory outcome."

But Holmes was by no means finished in his recollection of events.

"Miss Adler even left a sardonic note for me find in the place where she had secreted the photograph I was seeking to recover. The good Watson here chronicled the whole matter with an unsparing accuracy quite uncharacteristic of his accounts of my work and, and it remains, somewhat to my chagrin, one of my best-known cases."

"Your objections to my conclusion that that case ended well do you great credit, Mr Holmes," replied the King, "but I would reiterate that I was entirely satisfied with the outcome. Miss Adler was persuaded not to carry out her threat to send the photograph to my betrothed. That to me was better than the seizure of the photograph, and I would be pleased if I could consult with you again."

"Then, Your Majesty," said Holmes, putting his fingertips together, and drawing down the lids of his eyes so that they covered three quarters of his eyes, "pray consult."

"My subsequent marriage to Clotilde Lothman von Saxe-Meningen, second daughter of the King of Scandinavia, was concluded shortly after the Adler case. It was a brief affair. Within a year an unknown hand sent me a compromising picture of her enjoying the company of a courtier of lowly rank."

"Did the photographs date from after your marriage?"

"Certainly not. The association dated from well before I made her acquaintance."

"But you were by that time in wedlock. How were you able to dissolve your marriage?"

"You are perhaps not aware of the workings of the Roman Catholic church. After the expenditure of a significant sum from the royal purse, the marriage was annulled, and I was then once more a free man."

I was troubled by the inconsistency of the King's behaviour in terminating his marriage after receiving photographs of his wife in the company of another when he had himself been photographed in similar circumstances. I glanced across at Holmes whose face betrayed no sign of emotion, but a long silence ensued with the King perhaps awaiting a further question from Holmes.

Eventually the King, maybe reading the thoughts that were running through my head if not through the head of Holmes, flushed red, and broke the silence. "In this matter," he barked, "as in all others, my concern is only to preserve the honour my royal house."

"Quite so," soothed Holmes. "And presumably, having had your marriage annulled, you were then obliged to repay the dowry that your wife had brought, as an annulment means that there had never been a legal marriage and accordingly no dowry would be payable. Even for a royal purse, that, along with the monies you had to pay the Roman Catholic Church to secure your annulment, must have been a considerable burden."

There was another pause, shorter this time, and then the King went on speaking as though he had not heard Holmes's remark.

"I have remained a bachelor since that time. My royal duties are not very onerous, and, while I spend much time in Munich, I travel the world in search of its pleasures. But I have a responsibility to my kingdom to produce an heir who is both legitimate and male. The daughter, who was the result of what I must now regard as a mere dalliance with the Scandinavian King's second daughter, meets neither of these requirements. In these utilitarian times it is no longer an absolute requirement that I should marry someone of royal blood. I therefore decided to organise an exclusive ball here in London for a mixture of royalty and the most well-to-do eligible young ladies, and to choose from amongst them my future bride and a queen for my Bohemian realm."

"Pray continue."

"The ball was two nights ago. I did not know any of the people who attended as they had been invited by my secretary, but they had to show their invitations to the doormen to obtain admission to the ballroom at the Savoy Hotel where the ball was held. At about half-past-ten I became aware of a young lady, who had taken to the floor, whose beauty eclipsed that of all the other women present. I sent my secretary to bid her to come to me, and we danced together for some time."

"Did you speak to her while you danced?"

"We did speak a little, but I was too taken by her beauty to have much to say, or to remember much of what she said. I did not think even to ask her name."

"I see. Can you describe her?"

"She had the slenderest figure, golden hair, and piercing blue eyes. Her dress was a silver ball-gown."

"And what happened next?"

"At just before midnight I suggested a break in our dancing so that we could engage in more intimate colloquy. Just as I did so, the bells of St Martin in the Field's church in Trafalgar Square struck the hour. At their peel, my fair guest emitted a piecing shriek before exiting the ballroom with the greatest haste."

"How very singular. And what happened after that?"

"My footmen gave pursuit, but the lady disappeared around the corner of one of the long corridors in the hotel. When my footmen got to the corner, she had vanished from view."

"So you have nothing material left of this fair lady?"

"My footman found this dancing-shoe," replied the King, passing over a slipper of the utmost delicacy. "The young lady lost it in her flight. I read the deductions you made about Mr Henry Baker from his hat in the *Adventure of The Blue Carbuncle*, and I wondered if you could make similar inferences from this."

Holmes took the shoe to the light. Early in our acquaintance I would have been sceptical indeed about what he might infer from a single shoe about its wearer, but I knew to expect better now. My friend peered at it under a magnifying glass, turned it over several times, and then sniffed at the shoe's interior several times. He then handed it back to the King with a look of some puzzlement on his face.

"It is difficult," observed he, "to make deductions about an item of apparel that is being worn for the first time. This shoe had not been worn before the night of your ball."

My heart sank at what seemed to me to be a feeble excuse, but my friend had not finished.

"Nevertheless, it is clear that the shoe belongs to someone exceedingly well-to-do as it would not be possible to obtain such a shoe for less than three or four guineas. Note the fine stitching of the toe box to the welt. It is the work of a most able craftsman, yet one who has chosen to leave no trace of his identity. I can, I fear, deduce little about the physique of the wearer apart from the fact that she has a foot no larger a size two or three, and that she has closely cropped toe nails as there is no scratching from them on the inside of the toe which one would expect if the shoe's wearer had spent even the briefest time dancing."

"This is all very clear but none of this will be of much help in identifying the lady."

"And," continued Holmes, "she must have worn the shoe in a place where food is being prepared immediately before coming to your ball."

"So exquisite a lady is surely unlikely to have been in a place where food is prepared."

"Had food been served at your ball?"

"There had been champagne and oysters."

"The shoe is new, Your Majesty, yet it bears what appears under the lens of my glass to be a crushed pea on the forward outer corner of the heel. This was not an item of food that was served at your ball, and the shoe had not been worn at all before the ball. Therefore it must been put on its wearer's foot in a place where food was present and, as food being eaten is more likely to be on a plate than on the floor, it is more likely that the shoe was put on in a kitchen where food was being prepared."

"Does the shoe betray a nationality?" inquired our visitor. "You will understand that although I spoke to her in English, I would not be able to tell whether English was this lady's mother tongue or whether she was from overseas. Does the shoe perhaps give you an indication where it is manufactured?"

"There is nothing on it – no label, no maker's name, and no peculiarity of manufacture – to indicate a country of origin. That such a fine shoe should bear no such signs is a mystery indeed," replied my friend. "It is as if it appeared from nowhere."

He paused and then continued.

"And did you make no enquiries about the name the young lady gave when she entered the ball-room? One would assume that she must have had to show her invitation."

"My attendants had no idea of how she obtained entrance – the two doormen each stated that the other must have let her in. I suspect that they were each dazzled by her beauty just as I was, and so did not think to ask for an invitation..."

Our client's voice trailed away, and my friend lit his pipe before leaning back into his chair.

"So, we have no evidence to say where your guest came from, who she was, how she entered, how she left, or where she went to." A column of smoke rose from his pipe. It had risen almost to the ceiling before he spoke again. "Did your dance partner not tell you anything at all about herself?"

"My recollections are most vague. She said that she came from a city with no roads, and from that city's shoreline. She also said that the traffic ran differently where she came from than anywhere else in the country. She added that her father was a king who served kings – and, if it is possible, I would prefer a bride of royal blood."

"Anything else?"

"I fear I was flushed with passion and dancing; accordingly, I can remember little that would be of benefit to our discussion."

There was a long pause.

"Your Majesty," said my friend at last, "if I may summarise your petition, it is that you wish me to find the identity of the person who disappeared so precipitately at your ball. You are unable to furnish me with her name, but you have given me a description of her which defines her as female, young, slender, and fair. She has given you indications of where she might be from, but no city name. You have also recovered a shoe which had been worn by her, but this bears no name either of the wearer or of its maker. And it is brand new so hardly furnishes me with any data."

There was a pause as Holmes considered his next comment

"I fear, Your Majesty, I am a detective and not a magician," he said at last.

"My fair dancing partner to find, would I one of my provinces surrender," said our client plaintively. "Life bereft of someone of such a stamp is a grim prospect. Indeed, Mr Holmes, if you will not stir yourself to look into this matter, I may seek to employ somebody else."

Holmes raised his eyebrows at this threat, and immediately responded.

"Very well, Your Majesty, I shall look into the matter. I would bid you a good night."

We heard the King descend to the street.

"What an extraordinary affair!" I exclaimed, as his coach rattled away. "Are you sure you are wise to accept a commission when you have such slender information on which to base your investigation."

When I got no answer, I continued.

"What are to be your next steps, Holmes?"

"To smoke," answered he. "It is quite a three-pipe problem especially when the solution is so ob...." My friend broke off and I waited, agog to hear if he was going to say that the solution was "obvious", or "obscure." But when he next spoke, it was to say, "I beg that you do not speak to me for fifty minutes."

He curled himself up in his chair, with his thin knees drawn up to his hawk-like nose, and there he sat with his eyes closed and his black clay pipe thrusting out like the bill of some strange bird. I had quite concluded that he had dropped asleep, and indeed was nodding myself, for I was weary from my long day, when he suddenly sprang out of his chair and started pacing the room.

"So do you, Watson, have any insights you can bring to this case?"

My recent honeymoon had consisted of a tour of the cities of northern Italy and I wondered whether an answer might be found there. "Following the unification of Italy, the country still has kings from when it was a patchwork of independent states. And they retain their titles as king even though the Italian king is Victor Emanuel," I commented. "And in Venice," I continued, warming to my thesis, "where our tour concluded, there are no roads; every house is on a shoreline, and the traffic is all water-borne, and so goes differently from everywhere else in the country. On the Grand Canal, the water-borne transport even holds to the left whereas in the rest of Italy the traffic holds to the right. Could the mysterious woman's country be Italy and her city Venice where one of the former kings may have taken up residence?"

There was a pause and I wondered whether Holmes was going to respond with the dismissiveness that is so much his wont at the suggestions of others at solutions to the cases we investigate. Instead he visibly brightened.

"By Jove, Watson, you are coming on wonderfully well. I do fancy that a trip to Venice with the King might be the next step in this matter. When could you start?"

"You are asking **me** when I might start?" I responded, startled.

"Yes, I have a number of pressing cases on at present which are nearing their climax. I cannot leave the country. On the other hand, you have time on your hands to accompany the King."

"I am a newly married man who has just opened a medical practice," I retorted. "And I do not see that travelling to Venice in search of someone whose name is unknown to us is a profitable exercise."

"But your practice has only just opened, and you will barely be occupied while you wait for patients to come to your door. And I am sure that your wife, having just been with you for several weeks on honeymoon, would welcome a little time to herself rather than having you moping around the house while you wait for your practice to build."

"I do not mope," I replied curtly. "I have bought a failing practice which it will take all my energy to revive. And a young woman of elevated background is most unlikely to be seen by a member of the general public."

"Ah, but Venice is famous for the freedom of its society. And the King has a purse to open doors, and a heart that will press him to want to reach into that purse."

As is so often the way with Holmes, I allowed myself to be persuaded by him, and three days later I met the King at the Savoy Hotel.

Holmes's cases had already caused him to leave London, and the King and I were accordingly *à deux*. He was again attired as if a character from a fairy tale and was so well known a figure at the hotel that the head chef, Auguste Escoffier – all pristine overall and chef's hat – came to our table to advise us on the menu.

"I know His Royal Highness," said the famous chef, "is partial to game, and we have in today a haunch of venison fresh from the field."

"To Monsieur Escoffier's recommendations should one always pay heed!" exclaimed the King, and, after what was indeed a splendid lunch, the King and I repaired to Victoria Station to board the Golden Arrow to Paris, and thence the Orient Express to Venice. We passed through Lausanne and Milan on the way before we crossed the lagoon to Venice's Santa Lucia station.

We alighted, and, as a porter ran up to help us with our luggage, the King smiled for the first time. "I had forgotten that Venice is like nowhere else. All the world is here to enjoy itself." He nodded at a group of youngsters in high spirits although I noted one apparently young man in their party was in fact much older than he at first sight appeared and had daubed a thick layer of some sort of paste over himself to make himself look younger. A little further along the platform was an extended family sorting out their luggage. As well as adults and maids, there were five girls of all ages severely dressed in grey, and two lads in sailors' outfits who were engaged in an animated discussion. I heard what I took to be their names as we passed. "Janosh" it sounded like and "Tadiosh" and wondered at what language they might be speaking.

The King paused by them as though considering a matter. "It strikes me," said he, at last, "that the true shoreline of Venice is really the Lido – the sand bar that stands between the main part of Venice and the Adriatic. I shall take rooms at the Grand Hôtel des Bains. Come, I know where to get a water-taxi."

"But the Lido is motorised, and the road-traffic runs on the right," I objected, "so that does not fit with the clue of the traffic running differently from everywhere in Italy. By contrast every thoroughfare in the main part of Venice fits both that requirement and the requirement to be on the shoreline."

"I think you will find the Lido is the most fashionable part of Venice and so it is likeliest that my fair visitor came from there. And we can easily go from there into the centre of Venice. But come, we are tired. Let us make our way thither."

We emerged from the station, which stands at the edge of the historic part of Venice, to have our eyes assaulted by brilliant light. Some musicians had set up on the concourse that stands between Venice's station and the Grand Canal, but they had to compete with wheeling seagulls whose cries smote our ears, while the tang of brine hung in the air. But there was another smell which I could not place, and I asked the King what he thought it was.

"My dear fellow, we are right by a station, and the centre of Venice has ancient sanitation. It is to be expected that not all smells will be to our liking. That is another reason why I hope to be able to procure a room for us on the Lido where the air is fresher."

A half hour's water-taxi ride, and we were at the hotel. The King had obviously been a regular visitor at the Hotel des Bains, and we were greeted by the establishment's manager, Signor Visconti.

"It is truly a pleasure, *veramente un piacere*," he said to the King, "to see you here again, Your Majesty. We are very full at this time of year but of course we can find room for you and your companion, and everything will be arranged to make your stay as comfortable as possible. I wish you a pleasant stay."

"Could you ensure, Signor Visconti," said the King, "that both our rooms – *tutt' e due*," he emphasised in Italian, "command a sea view."

"I will see to the matter myself," said Visconti, and made a note. "**Both** rooms."

Before dinner I strolled the hotel's magnificent grounds. There were gazebos with views out to sea, a knot garden, a series of splendid fountains, and sporting facilities including a croquet lawn, bowling green, and tennis courts. It was hot, and I noticed the same peculiar smell that had wafted round the station. In the end I went down to the sandy beach although the smell was present there too, and I soon repaired to the hotel's dining room.

As we ate, I tried to engage King Wilhelm in discussion on how we would conduct the search. "Your idea of booking us into this hotel is the correct one," I conceded. "If your visitor is wealthy enough to know her way around the London Savoy, then she is likely to be seen in this, the most fashionable part of the city."

But the King seemed distracted and stared over my shoulder round the dining room. In the end I looked round to see what he might be looking at, but the scene behind us of well-dressed diners partaking of their evening meal was ordinary enough. I noticed among the guests sat the family that we had seen at the station. "They are Polish," said my dinner companion when I pointed this out. "I have spoken to them, and they are called Moes."

"That name does not sound very Polish," remarked I.

"Bohemia, and Poland to the north, are a patchwork of languages – German among the educated people, but amongst the peasantry you hear Czech, Moravian, Sorb, Lach, and in the north of Bohemia, and, of course, across Poland, Polish. As King of Bohemia, I have to speak something of all of them."

"But guests here are hardly peasants," I objected.

"Indeed not," said the King, "I imagine they are from the Polish aristocracy. I met plenty of people like them when I lived in Warsaw where I met the fair Irene Adler. My knowledge of the Polish tongue came in very useful then." He paused and then spoke in a hushed tone.

"Now, Miss Adler was the daintiest thing under a bonnet. And she had the finest, most boyish figure. Ah, if only she were here."

And he continued to stare pointedly over my shoulder. He seemed as if in a reverie from which I was unable to divert him. In the end I withdrew to my room although the King seemed barely to notice my departure.

When I rose the next day, the King was nowhere to be found. In the end I asked the concierge who suggested I look on the beach. There sat the King, serene as could be. He was seated on a wicker chair looking quite dapper with a fresh flower in his lapel as he looked out to the Adriatic. Further down the beach I could see the youngsters of the Moes family playing a variety of games. The girls played board-games at a fold-up table while the two lads, the swarthy Janos and the much fairer Tadzio – the King had told me were their names – were engaged in friendly horseplay.

"I thought I would sit on the beach in case the fair love of my heart chanced to venture onto it," said the King.

"But surely we should be asking people if they know of any woman of standing here who matches your description," I responded.

"Ah dear doctor," replied the King, "this is the place in Venice where all the quality people come. If my love is in Venice, it is here where we will renew our acquaintance."

"Having come all this way," I commented, "it is surely worth our while buying the local *gazzetta* and seeing who the gossip pages are talking about. We may even find a photograph of the local celebrities. Or," I said, a happy thought striking me, "we could employ a local detective to see if he can find out whether a local beauty was at a recent ball in London."

"Good doctor, these are all excellent ideas," replied the King. "Here is my purse," he added, passing me over what was in fact a heavy chamois bag. "Feel free to use it as you see fit - whether to buy the local paper or to employ a private investigator. I shall stay here and enjoy the view."

I went back to the hotel.

On my way I found that a Gypsy band – tall dark types playing violins, guitars, mandolins, and fifes and accompanying a singer – had been allowed to set up in the grounds. Their smocks and hats made a most colourful sight although their music-making, particularly that of their squat vocalist, left much to be desired. I soon stopped watching and went to the foyer. I changed some money at the reception of the hotel, and in the lofty atrium I noticed again the peculiar odour I had smelt at the station on the previous day and, if truth be told, everywhere I had gone to in Venice. In the atrium the smell was modified by the additional smell of paint as an overalled brushman worked away.

I spoke to the concierge about it.

"Ah Dr Watson," he soothed in good but heavily accented English, "It is the scirocco. It is the wind from the southeast. It comes from the Sahara and brings rain mixed with red sand from the desert. We call it *la pioggia rossa* or red rain because it is the colour of *sangue*." He paused as he cast about in his mind for the English word. "It is the colour of blood."

"The smell is of a wind?" I questioned, as the smell, to my nose, was not of a natural product.

"No, no sir," said the concierge, "the smell is of disinfectant. The wind is said to be damaging to the health and so we spray everywhere. It is a precaution we take every time the scirocco blows. And we try and hide the smell as you see, by having Gustavo there do some painting."

As I headed out of the hotel to the vaporetto stop, I crossed paths with the King. "I am heading to the barbers," he said, although his meagre head of grizzled hair seemed in no need of a trim. "Good luck in your search."

There is a vaporetto that does nothing but shuttle to and fro between St Mark's Square and the Lido. In ten minutes, I was on St Mark's Square.

Despite what I had said, I had formed no precise view of where I might go to prosecute my investigation and, in the end, decided to go to the British consulate. I am sure as plain Dr John Watson, I would not have obtained any sort of audience with such a vague petition as I had, but my association with Mr Sherlock Holmes soon got me in front of the under-secretary, Mr Britten.

"Your missing person's enquiry," said the suave official, "is certainly like nothing I have heard before, but here is a listing of the leading families who are resident in Venice showing where they live and the occupants of their houses. You are right to suspect that many of them are on the Lido."

I confess I could barely believe my fortune in obtaining such a listing.

"May I ask why you hold such a document?" I asked.

"We represent Great Britain here," said Britten. "It is of course a coincidence that my name is the same as the country I represent, but I feel I embody my country's interests. His Majesty's government needs to know who the most important people are in order to prosecute its own policies."

I decided to go back to the Lido to show the King the fruits of my visit to the main part of Venice and returned to the St Mark's vaporetto station. I just missed a vaporetto which had come from the Lido and left to go back there just before I got to the stop. I nodded to the Moeses, who had been on it, and whom I now passed. As I waited on the quay for a vaporetto to take me back to the Lido, the water-taxi of the Grand Hotel de Bains drew up. On it was the King who seemed to have undergone something of a transformation. His whole mien radiated energy, he had dressed himself modishly, and he had had his hair rather obviously dyed. He saw me and said, "I am keen to see the sights of Venice once more. At my age, one never knows how often one will have the chance to see them again."

"I have some excellent material for our invest...," I began.

"This evening at the hotel," came the reply from the King, as he strode purposefully past me.

When I returned to the hotel it struck me that Signor Visconti might know some of the families on the list Britten had given me. Visconti knew my association with Holmes, and I decided to take him a little way into my confidence.

"I am here to conduct an enquiry into a missing person," I intimated. "I am looking for a young lady of wealth – so, I assume, the daughter of one of the rich families. We suspect she is Venetian. We do not know her name, but she is known to have been in London last week."

"Many of the wealthiest families from Venice itself and, *in fatti*, from across the Veneto," said Visconti thoughtfully, "come to this establishment for family celebrations. They sometimes ask for us to organise pictures of the gathering, and I generally supervise the photography myself as I am a keen amateur photographer, as was my father. I keep back some of the photographs that are the less successful ones out of those taken to see what went wrong. Why not come back with your companion and he can take a look."

"That sounds most promising," I said, thinking that even Holmes might be impressed that I seemed to have two lines of inquiry.

I wondered how I might fill the time until the King returned and thought of prospecting the list of names given to me by the under-secretary at the consulate might be the way forward. I asked if I might borrow the hotel's gazetteer. "With the greatest pleasure, Dr Watson," came the reply from the concierge. "Here it is. You will find here every *piazza, piazzetta*, alleyway or *calle*, as we call them."

"Not many roads or *strade* here," I responded, eager to show off one of the few words of Italian that I knew.

"Indeed not, dottore. Venice is in every way a rule unto itself."

I took the list from the British consulate and the gazetteer into the hotel's lounge. I sat noting down the addresses of major families in Venice and their family members. I confess I felt rather like Holmes as he had sat compiling lists of possible suspects from registers of crew members at Lloyds Registry at the time of the *Adventure of the Five*

Orange Pips. The list Britten had given me disclosed details of individual family members, sometimes with dates of birth, so I was able to identify seven names which met the parameters of age and gender. I then matched the addresses to the gazetteer and found that no fewer than four of the families lived within a mile of the hotel's grand front-entrance.

I was sufficiently pleased with my progress that I decided to seek out the King and went to the hotel reception to see if he had returned. The receptionist smiled when he saw me. "His Majesty returned twenty minutes ago. He declared the intention of going to the tennis courts as he said he has an interest in the game."

I turned around and headed out towards the gardens.

The Gypsy band, whose music had been so inharmonious previously, had now stationed itself at the foot of the stairs leading down to the grounds. They seemed to have dispensed with their croaking singer and were led instead by a man playing a fife and by a lean fiddler – both clothed in apparel as exotic as the plumage of a parrot. Quite in contrast to their previous performance, they now poured out a stream of untamed and bewitching melodies.

I was not alone in being entranced, and soon a large crowd had assembled to listen. The pipe player seemed never to draw a breath as the music bubbled like a spring in spate from under his fingers, and the violinist, no less a talent, appended a cadenza where he brought his fingers up to only a straw's breadth from the bridge. It was the fiddler who introduced each piece in an English accented as though it were Italian – first a siciliano, then a tarantella, then something that to me was not even a name – as the whole panoply of Italian folk music was laid before us.

After another particularly virtuosic dance melody, the violinist and the pipe player started walking among the crowd proffering their hats to collect money.

At the parents of the Polish family, the hat slipped out of the violinist's hand, and the father helped him to pick it up. Then he got to me. As I reached out to put some coins into it, the hat again slipped out of his grasp, and some coins rolled to the floor. As I bent down to help the violinist pick them up, I heard an incisive whisper in a familiar voice. "Pack your bags and meet me at the reception in fifteen minutes."

It was only by staring hard after the roughly clad figure, who, once the coins had been picked up, proceeded to collect money from the row of spectators behind without another glance at me that I realized that it was indeed Sherlock Holmes who had spoken to me.

So vehemently expressed an instruction was one I was disinclined to ignore, and in less than the time stated I had my bags packed, and was in the reception where Holmes, now as conservatively attired as if he were back at Baker Street, was already waiting for me.

"The investigation is complete," he said. "We must to London post-haste."

"But I have only just got the names and addresses of the lead..." I began

But suddenly, there was a commotion as one of the garden staff, in fact, Gustavo, the man whom I had previously seen painting in the foyer, dashed in and said something to the receptionist who immediately called Visconti who approached me.

"Dottore Watson! Your friend, the King of Bohemia has collapsed by the tennis court. We need your services as a doctor."

"Our train from Santa Lucia is in an hour," I heard Holmes say, but I was not be kept from ministering to anyone in distress.

We headed for the tennis court but when we got there it was obvious the King was beyond medical help. There was no pulse when I put my fingers to his wrist although his face bore a look of seraphic calm rather than being pulled into the contorted state common in cases of sudden death. Although I did make every effort to revive him, life had passed from his body.

"Heart failure," I said grimly.

A group of people including Gustavo had come with us. I know that Holmes, from his love of opera, spoke Italian, and I asked him to ask the attendant if he had seen what happened. The dialogue that follows is presented as a straight conversation between the garden attendant and me although it flowed through the medium of Holmes's translation.

"I was planting birds of paradise in the bed outside the wire of the tennis court. Two lads were inside playing tennis, and the man who has died was watching them closely from outside the court."

"Do you know which lads?" I asked.

"One was fair, and one was dark, but I do not have much to do with hotel guests, so I do not know their names."

"What happened next?"

"They had an argument about where a ball had landed. They were looking at a mark in the sand when the dark boy struck the fair boy and knocked him down. The man who had been watching them play and rose from out of his seat – I assume to go to the aid of the fair boy. But there was no need as the blond boy got up. But the dark boy knocked him down again before stalking off. The fair boy rose again, turned around, and looked at the gentlemen who was still standing but then fell back into his seat. The blond boy then ran off. And then I saw that the gentleman had slumped right down into his seat. I went over to him and said, 'Signor?' When he failed to move, I ran to the reception."

Holmes thanked Gustavo and he, Visconti, and I went back into the hotel.

"Well, it is perhaps as well," said Holmes.

"What is 'as well'?" I asked but Holmes would not be drawn further.

When we got back to reception, Holmes insisted on checking whether the Orient Express was running on time and, when he found that it was late, prevailed upon Visconti to summon the hotel's motor-launch to get us to the train station on time to catch it.

As we waited for the launch to arrive, Holmes asked Visconti if the hotel needed any signature from me on my departure.

Visconti handed over the guest book and I signed my name against the signature I had provided on my arrival. To my surprise, Holmes leant over my shoulder as I did this, and knocked over the inkpot that spilt over the page obliterating the entries.

"You are obviously still very shaken, Watson," said he. "But here is the motor-launch. As the King has paid for your room, there is, in any case, no need to provide a signature."

It was only once we were across the lagoon and heading for Milan that Holmes lit his pipe and said, "Watson, I fear I owe you something of an apology."

"I was on my way to finding a suitable list of wealthy Venetian ladies who might have been at the King's ball," I expostulated, "and you ordered me to leave Venice just as I was about to approach the King with it."

I told Holmes about the progress of my investigation and he listened with an engagement quite uncharacteristic of him. "I had found seven families in Venice which were of sufficient wealth to have had made a trip to London and who had a daughter of the right age to match the King's description of the young lady at the ball," I concluded.

"Ah, the investigation about the lady at the ball," he said when I had finished. "No, there was never a mystery about that, but the association with the King might have been ruinous for your reputation, and your continued sojourn in Venice might have been ruinous for your health."

The previous paragraph contains no fewer than three important statements all of which left me at a complete loss; I asked Holmes to explain.

"There is a cholera epidemic in Venice – that is the reason for the pervasive smell. Disinfectant is being sprayed everywhere to try and limit its impact. News of it has got into the international press although it has been kept out of the local newspapers for fear of scaring off tourists."

"But surely you did not need to come all the way to Venice in person and disguise yourself as a street-musician to tell me that? A telegram from Baker Street would have sufficed."

"I fear my original enthusiasm about your trip to Venice was because I wanted the King in a known place a long way from London and under the eye of someone I trusted. I needed to carry out an investigation into his original story about which I had the gravest doubts."

"You did not believe that the ball of which he spoke had actually taken place?"

"No, I disbelieved that he would have had the resources to live the life-style that he was leading if he had had to pay back the dowry which he received for his marriage to the second daughter of the King of Scandinavia as well as paying the Roman Catholic Church for an annulment. Returning the dowry would have been a crippling sum even to a royal purse, and getting an annulment was likely to be even more costly. Yet he had a well upholstered pocket if he could pay for a ball at the Savoy, let alone if he travelled the world seeking its pleasures as he suggested was his modus vivendi."

"So how did you investigate his affairs?"

"The day after our interview with the King, I travelled to Stockholm and obtained an audience with the King of Scandinavia for whom I have had the honour of performing some services in the past. He told me that his daughter had instigated the separation because of the unnatural preferences of the King of Bohemia which you saw sign of in Venice."

"Unnatural preferences?"

"Dear Watson, did you fail to observe his interest in Tadzio, the Polish boy? He was trailing him around everywhere."

I am sure my face showed my complete astonishment at my friend's statement, and he continued.

"The King of Scandinavia would not be drawn into specific details on the behaviour of his fellow monarch but knowing that there was some peculiarity about it put me in to a very difficult moral position."

"So you asked me to travel to Venice with the Bohemian King who you thought had unnatural desires so that you could carry out a separate investigation into him?" I asked, appalled at what I had been dragged away from my wife to participate in.

"I did all I could to minimise the time you spent away from your home. I went straight to Stockholm and then straight from Stockholm to Venice to carry out my investigation. On arrival in Venice I immediately joined one of the troupes of musicians who are to be found everywhere in the city as I felt I had to observe the King's behaviour from close quarters. Dressed in exotic garb and playing my violin, I soon formed a view of where his true interests lie. I needed to warn the Moeses and, in fact, I was able to do so, as you saw, when disguised as a street musician."

"What did you say to them?"

"I told them about the cholera epidemic in Venice and that they should leave for the good of themselves and their children."

"You could not tell them the truth about the risk to their son?"

"Nothing specific had happened and making accusations about a man's interest in children is the most serious accusation one can make of anyone. I could not do so without proofs and wanted to avoid the King giving me opportunities to obtain proofs. Telling them about the cholera epidemic enabled me to warn them to leave Venice without casting aspersions on the King."

"But he would have tried the same thing with someone else. If you had these suspicions, you needed to tell someone in authority."

"His death has obviated the need for that but going to the Venetian authorities to make such a grave accusation against a monarch when nothing had actually happened would have been a most hazardous undertaking."

He broke off and drew heavily on his pipe before continuing.

"And I had to ensure your association with him was terminated abruptly. Hence our precipitate departure from Venice and my destruction of the evidence at the hotel that you had stayed there."

My feelings, as my reader may imagine, remained a mixture of anger at Holmes for having me make a trip to Venice which he knew would be fruitless, wonder at myself for not drawing any inferences about the King's lack of interest in my investigation, and concern that harm might have come to young Tadzio.

I put the latter point to Holmes.

"From your description of events, nothing has happened. The King's situation was a little like that of a pyromaniac. It is not an offence to have the inclination to light fires – an offence is only committed if the pyromaniac acts on his inclination. And, as I said at the hotel, nothing now can happen. I would not exclude the possibility of previous offences in the past, but I have no evidence that any such accusation has ever been levelled against him."

Holmes and I were faced with twenty-four hours in close confinement on three trains and a ship. Over this time my anger at Holmes for sending me on what he knew to be a fool's errand rose and fell.

Holmes defended himself robustly.

"There was something in the King's story that made no sense. I had to satisfy myself that it was not so untoward that it would be irresponsible if I identified the person who, he said, was the object of his desiring. How better to keep the various options open than to have you keep an eye on him while I carried out my investigation?"

I suspect that my reader will now be most interested in the identification of the lady who had attended the King's ball, gave the King such ambiguous clues about her identity, and then so abruptly disappeared, and I put this to Holmes as we finally drew into Victoria Station.

"If you would care to come to Baker Street tomorrow, I can resolve that for you over lunch." He replied. "I feel I owe you as much."

I arrived at 221 b on the next day expecting to be faced with Mrs Hudson's solid fare. Instead a hansom stood before the door into which we climbed.

As we went east along the Marylebone Road, Holmes, rather to my surprise, as he had never shown an interest in local history, started to provide a commentary on the route. "So, we here leave Marylebone Road and head further east onto the Euston Road. This whole road system, along with Pentonville Road, was originally known as the New Road. But it was realised that it was impractical to have so long a road with a single name in a rapidly growing city, and the different sections were given separate names."

"And now south down Tottenham Court Road," he added a few minutes later, before saying, "we are now at the southern end of Charing Cross Road and arriving at the northeast corner of Trafalgar Square. Here we are right on the edge of the old city of London. St Martin in the Fields church which you see on your left was so called because it stood in fields outside the city walls."

We turned left into the Strand.

"And now we are within the boundaries of the old city of London," said Holmes. "And the Strand marks the old shoreline of the city. Within the city's ancient walls there are no thoroughfares referred to as a road – only as streets, lanes, alleys, yards, and squares – because the word 'road' was not in common usage in medieval times when the old city of London was first built."

As ever with Holmes, I wondered why I had not realised that the true import of the clues which we had been given.

"And now we turn right from the Strand and into Savoy Place," continued Holmes. "You will note, Watson, that uniquely among British streets, in Savoy Place the traffic drives on the right."

We went into the restaurant of the Savoy where Holmes had booked a table. We had barely sat down, when Auguste Escoffier came out of the kitchen.

"I received your note this morning, Mr Holmes."

"Monsieur Escoffier, Watson," said my friend turning to me, "is known as king of chefs and the chef of kings. So, he is a king who serves kings as the heads of every royal house in Europe are enthusiastic consumers of his cuisine. He has published the recipes of five sauces that are the staple of every noble kitchen." Holmes turned to the chef who beamed at these words of praise. "I mentioned it was to your third child, your daughter Germaine, I wanted to speak. You may, by all means, stay here while we talk to her."

As Monsieur Escoffier went to get his daughter, Holmes explained, "Monsieur Escoffier has been lived at this hotel for many years and I was able to find out his family's records through the last census – not unlike how you approached the case in Venice, good Watson."

A few minutes later, Mademoiselle Escoffier appeared. My reader will be used to the female characters in my stories being the fairest members of the fairer sex but this one – with tumbling golden locks, piercing blue eyes, and the slenderest frame – outshone them all, yet for all that she looked barely seventeen.

"Tell me about your appearance at the ball here last week," said Holmes.

"There is not much to tell," said Mademoiselle Escoffier in a soft clear voice with perfect but charmingly accented English. "I was determined to go to that ball even though I realised that the guests were beyond my station. Many of the guests at the ball were spending the night here and several had brought more than one ball gown and the other accoutrements for a ball. I am friendly with one of the people in housekeeping and so was able to gain access to the rooms of some of the guests."

She turned to look at her father whose face was a mixture of pride in the resourcefulness of his daughter and concern about what further revelations might follow.

"The doormen had been provided by the hotel so I knew they would raise no objection when I entered the ballroom, and I told them to blame each other if my admission caused any problems. I was unsurprised that the King singled me out for his attention, but I found his conversation most disagreeable. He seemed far more interested in my being his *maîtresse* when I had thought he was looking for a wife."

She tossed her head back in derision.

"Nevertheless, I danced with him, as I love to dance. But his attempts at conversation became more and more" she broke off to search for a word, "*degueulasse…*," she finally added.

"She means distasteful," interrupted the young lady's father.

"Until at just before midnight he said he would like to see me dress as a boy and made another suggestion that nothing *…rien, rien, rien…*. will induce me to repeat." She paused, apparently overcome by her revulsion at whatever the King had proposed.

It was a full minute before she spoke again.

"I ran in disgust from the ballroom, and, to make sure that I could not be followed, shot down a laundry chute which is concealed in a wall in the corridor. When I got to the bottom, I found I had lost a shoe, but I returned everything else to where it came from."

"We were unable to account for why the shoe had no maker's name."

"My entire outfit belonged to Princess Beatrice of Saxe-Coburg and Gotha, a grand-daughter of the last queen," said Mademoiselle Escoffier, apparently somewhat taken aback by our ignorance of the ways of royalty. "The royal family, of course, has its shoes made for it by hand by its own shoemaker who, as he works for the King, does not put a name into the shoes. I actually took two pairs of shoes from the princess's bedroom as I was not sure which suited my dress better, and finally put on the pair which I decided I liked best in the kitchen."

Mademoiselle Escoffier answered this last question with another coquettish toss of the head, and Holmes turned to me. "As my biographer, are there any other questions you would wish to ask Mademoiselle Escoffier?"

"No indeed," I said, quite breathless both at the young lady's beauty and her poise, "I feel that Mademoiselle Escoffier has an answer for everything."

"In that case," said Holmes, "perhaps, Monsieur Escoffier, you might like to see if you have any more venison left. Dr Watson has been unstinting in his praise for what you served him last time."

"You see Watson," said Holmes, as we finished our meal, "it was obvious to me from the first that whoever had caught the King's eye must have had an intimate knowledge of the hotel. Otherwise how could they get pass the doormen to get in, and how else could a lady in a ball-dress disappear completely when pursued hot-foot by two footmen?"

"That is clear to me," I said, "but why did you need to me to accompany the King to Venice when you knew the object of his desires was not there?"

"I had my suspicions about the King's story, but I could not deprive the young lady for whom he had expressed such ardent interest the opportunity of becoming a royal bride without substantiating those suspicions. It therefore suited me to have the King well away from London, and your suggestion of Venice, on which I must commend you for it met all the criteria set by the King's recollection of his conversation with Mademoiselle Escoffier, enabled me to do that."

"And what is to happen now?"

"The King of Bohemia will be succeeded by his daughter. The Roman Catholic Church's canon law court in Bohemia took a less dim view of Princess Clotilde's complaint than I do and rejected it as grounds for an annulment. She instigated a divorce in the civil courts, and so the King retained his dowry, and their daughter remained legitimate in the eyes of the church. Although the King and his wife had lived separate lives for many years, there is no legal impediment to a female heir."

There was a silence.

"It seems to me, Holmes," I said at last, "that in this case you have acted for the well-being of the public and have largely ignored your client's original petition."

"Although the King of Scandinavia was very cautious in what he said, I took the view that I would have to learn more about the King of Bohemia before I acted on the latter's behalf. Given the predilections that I found he had, I am pleased that I did so, and I am pleased that I took steps to ensure that our association with the whole matter is unlikely to come to light."

He paused and relit his pipe. Suddenly he looked care-worn in a way I had never seen in all our long friendship.

"Any such association is ruinous," he said at last. "You may note that I ended my connection with the Baker Street Irregulars almost as soon as you started publishing accounts of our adventures. I knew you would publish more stories about me, and I could not take the risk that anyone would make unfounded suggestions. That is also why I have done my best to destroy any trace that either of us have been in the company of the King. This story too must wait for publication until long after we have both departed this vale of tears."

An Encirclement Thwarted

It has long been a matter of speculation among my readers why *His Last Bow* should contain so many departures from the style used in the rest of the works which my friend, Mr Sherlock Holmes, allowed to be published in his lifetime.

It bears a subtitle, *The War Service of Sherlock Holmes*, it is told in the third person when it could, with only very minor modification, have been told in the first person with me adopting my customary role as narrator, and Holmes taunts the malefactor he apprehends.

Although none of these features on their own make the story unique, taken together they do indeed mark this narrative out.

In fact, Holmes's war service before the Great War had a much wider remit than was disclosed in *His Last Bow*, and the following reveals for the first time one of the many other matters in which he was involved. The anomalies of style and content in *His Last Bow* were included, as my reader may by now have guessed, at the suggestion of the British government. As Mr Asquith, who was Prime Minister at the time, and who plays a major role in the rest of this narrative, put it, "If speculation is rife about the narrative voice, the use of a subtitle, and Mr Holmes's behaviour towards the criminal in your story, Dr Watson, there might be less speculation as to what else he might have been doing in the service of his country at its time of peril."

The story that follows also explains why nothing more is heard of Inspector Gregson after the case of *The Red Circle* and draws heavily on one of Holmes's monographs. My reader will be aware of my friend's contribution to the specialist literature on tobacco ash, tattoos, beekeeping, medieval music, footprints, and codes to which he refers without expanding. Some or all of these may be included in further accounts of his adventures, but in this work it is my friend's monograph on codes which emerges as the magnum opus of the genre that it is.

It was eight o'clock in the evening of that day of infamy – Sunday the 28th of June 1914 – when there was a tap on our door. I was at that time in practice although my surgery was closed at such an hour. I answered the door myself and, standing on the doorstep, was Sherlock Holmes. He still cut the tall lean figure of his heyday but had a goatee beard for which he made a slightly shame-faced apology.

"I am in the service of the country, dear Watson, and even my smooth chin must be sacrificed in its cause."

I would characterise the friendship between Holmes and me in the years leading up to the first German war as sporadic though warm. He occasionally came to our house in Queen Square where I had my practice when he needed accommodation in London, but I otherwise saw him seldom.

"I am delighted to see you, my dear fellow," I said, throwing wide the door.

"And I you, Watson. Could you put me up for one night?"

"Of course, my friend," said I, "but what brings you to London?"

"I received at my bee-keeper's cottage this afternoon a telegram from the prime minister. He suggested we meet here as he would like to conduct a meeting away from the fevered atmosphere of Westminster."

"Are you able to tell me what it is he wished to discuss?"

"I would be reluctant to speculate on matters of state other than to say it can only be something very grave that would cause him to seek my counsel at such short notice. He will be here at nine, and I would welcome the presence of my Boswell at the meeting."

At nine o'clock sharp, there was another knock on the door, and I found myself greeting on the door-step, not only the plump and slightly puffy-faced Mr Asquith, but also a tawny-bearded man, whom the Prime Minister presented to us as Mr Gregson, but whom Holmes and I knew by his old police rank as Inspector Gregson, and whom we had last seen in the story *The Red Circle*.

Asquith spoke first.

"Gentleman, what I am about to say will not yet be known to you, but it will be on the front page of every newspaper tomorrow. Today has seen the assassination of the Austrian crown-prince, Archduke Franz-Ferdinand and of his wife, Sophie, as they were driving in an open-topped car in the Bosnian capital, Sarajevo."

"This is a very grave matter, Prime Minister," said my friend, "but how can I help you in this? This is surely the responsibility of the Bosnian authorities."

"The assassins, although not perhaps all those behind the assassins, were arrested at the scene of the crime. But the assassination has much wider ramifications. Europe is a powder keg.

One spark could cause an explosion, and this could be it. At the same time, the military strengths of the Entente powers – the Russians, the French and us on the one hand – and of the Central powers – Germany, Austria, and Turkey on the other – are evenly matched. Never has a small advantage to one side been of greater leverage."

"You make yourself plain, Prime Minister, but you surely have not convened this meeting just to tell me this."

"Indeed so, Mr Holmes. Something else has arisen at the same time the investigation of which is more obviously suited to your talents. I cannot believe this other matter is unrelated to today's assassination, but I will leave it to Mr Gregson to elaborate."

"You will recall, Mr Holmes," began Gregson, "our work together in the 1880s and 1890s. As Inspector Gregson, I was present at many of your greatest triumphs – *A Study in Scarlet, The Greek Interpreter*, and – the last time we saw each other – *The Red Circle*. In that last case, you decoded a message between the main players in the investigation which had a key part in unravelling the matter. I was so impressed by your work, that I was inspired to read your monograph on ciphers, *A Qualitative Study of Replacement Code Creation and Decryption with Observations on Best Practices for Code Security and Code Breaking*, to which you refer in *The Dancing Men*. I thought your slim volume was of extraordinary interest, not only because you elucidated one-hundred and sixty ciphers which turn letters into a code, but also because of its additional observations."

I could see that Holmes was pleased by this encomium and Gregson continued.

"Shortly after reading your work, I was recruited by the British Secret Service, and I am now plain Mr Gregson, although for some of my work I go under a variety of names. I have learnt languages – German, French, and Russian among others – and have acquired skills in advanced mathematics and in semiotics to enhance my code-breaking capabilities. But I have a most urgent coding matter I am unable to resolve, and it is on this I would wish to talk to you now."

"Pray continue."

"The assassination of which the prime minster has spoken occurred at a quarter past ten this morning Bosnian time. The news was telegraphed around the world, and we know that it was received in Berlin within the hour. An hour after that, our source in the Berlin war ministry gave his British handler a piece of paper, with the information that the text on it was a coded message that was being passed to all German military missions on the continent of Europe."

"And what was the coded message?"

"It was terse in the extreme – I have it here."

Gregson passed Holmes a piece of paper on which was written the following, "952, 395, 239, 523".

Holmes sat poised over the slip of paper with these four numbers on. It was quite five minutes before he put it down on the table and looked up. He opened his mouth to speak, but paused to pick it up again, and then he studied it for another five minutes. When he eventually spoke, it was in a voice shorn of its normal incisiveness.

"And how does this compare with other German codes you have seen?"

"German codes are normally replacement codes – so one symbol or number, or character-set as we call them, replaces a letter."

"And how do you decrypt them?"

"We are aware of four different codes, three of which they have introduced in the last five years. In principle they are no more and no less complex than our own replacement codes. But the Germans are obviously not devotees of your monograph on codes as their use of them breaches fundamental rules of code security."

"Perhaps you would explain."

"They use codes to send messages which need not be coded whereas you said that messages should only be coded if their security is paramount. Thus, we broke one code because we noted a large amount of telegraph traffic at the end of January last year with messages ending with an exclamation mark. We soon worked out that messages were being sent to mark the Kaiser's birthday on the 27th of January."

"Anything else?"

"They take no steps to conceal the use of the letter 'e' – much the most common letter in English, French, German, and Italian. You used that flaw in the code employed in *The Dancing Men* to decipher messages sent by Abe Slaney to the woman he was seeking to woo, and we have done the same to their codes. So, as you identified that a man with his arms raised 𝋌 must represent the letter 'E' as it appeared twice in a short message addressed to the lady in the case, Elsie Cubitt, so we look out for repeated characters in messages. Once we have identified what character set represents the letter 'e,' we are well on the way to cracking the code."

"And?"

"They ignore your dictum that the carriage of a coded message should be accorded the same security as the equivalent message in plain text. We find it easy to get hold of their messages and to replace them so that their abstraction is not noticed. We do not make the same mistakes with our own messages."

"Perhaps you could expand on the measures you take with you own codes."

"We accord coded messages the same security as if an uncoded version of the same information were being sent, we only code when essential, we frequently send messages that are written in one code and then translated into another, and it is a requirement of our codes that they use a different character or character-set to code each successive use of the letter 'e'."

"You are, if I may make so bold, Mr Gregson, a model student of my work."

Gregson flushed with pleasure at this rare word of praise from Holmes.

"And what do you make of this code?" asked Holmes.

"It provides none of the clues we normally use to unlock codes, Mr Holmes. It is of only four characters and none repeat themselves. If it refers to events in Sarajevo, there is no obvious means of identifying the events or the location."

"Could it be a pre-arranged set of characters to trigger a particular action?"

"That may be so Mr Holmes – indeed a message with only four character-sets could hardly be anything else – but that still leaves this code uncracked and does not tell us what action is being taken."

Gregson's voice tailed off uncertainly and Asquith took over.

"We were wondering whether your schedule would permit you to try to decipher this code, Mr Holmes."

Holmes looked at the message, "As you say, it is hard indeed to think what meaning it could convey in so short a span as four character-sets. All four of the sets consist of three numbers ranging in size from 239 to 932. This means that multiple numbers may in a future coded message reflect the same letter. This will make decryption far harder than would normally be the case."

There was another long pause.

Holmes straightened up, and I could see from his face that he had no solution.

"Gentlemen, I cannot reason without material. I fear I am unable to give you any suggestions on the text you have given me save to say that it must be of major import if the Germans should choose this day of all days to introduce a new code. I would bid you to bring me any new messages of this three-number character-set type, but on the data that you have given to me this evening, I am not in a position to offer any solutions at this time."

The mood among the four of us was sombre indeed. Asquith rose to leave, and Gregson followed him. Holmes and I walked our visitors to the door, and Asquith had already gone from the step down onto the street when an insight seemed to strike him, and he turned back.

"Mr Holmes," he said, "you have a completely free hand to solve this matter."

"Prime Minister, I fear that there are other matters on which I am working on, which you know about," said Holmes, ruefully stroking his goatee beard, "which will preclude me dedicating any significant time to decrypting this code."

There was a pause and I could see that the Prime Minister was wrestling with a dilemma.

"I would reiterate what I just said," he replied at last. "You have *carte blanche*. Do whatever you may wish to do and use any resources you see fit to use to crack this code. And you may, Mr Holmes," he continued, "be candid to Dr Watson and Mr Gregson about your work for British Intelligence. Dr Watson is known from all his previous work to be trustworthy, and it is conceivable we may need him as a witness in a trial at some point. And for your investigation into this new code you may need to avail yourself of the help of Mr Gregson here, and I can hardly expect him to do your bidding if he is not informed of your other activities. I must return to Downing Street. I cannot be absent from my post for any significant length of time at this country's moment of peril."

After the Prime Minister had departed, at Holmes's suggestion Gregson came back into the house, and my friend told him and me about his counter espionage work under the alias of Altamont with the German spymaster, Count von Bork. "I pose as a disaffected Irish-American," he said, "to give false information about British military preparedness and dispositions. And I have unmasked German spies in the highest British political and military circles." He puffed out smoke from his pipe as he so often did in his moments of triumph. "My work is entering its critical phase, and I cannot spare time for an investigation into enemy coded messages which would require my skills to be used for interception of messages as well for their decryption. Thus, Gregson, I would ask you to use your resources to track down messages in this new code, but I will make myself available, as far as I can, if you want any help in cracking them."

After Gregson's eventual departure, Holmes and I remained up late. He sat hunched over the piece of paper and addressed no word to me as he stared down. I puffed my pipe until half-past eleven. As I went to sleep, I could still hear Holmes pacing his room across the corridor.

It was at half-past four in the morning when I heard a furious pounding at the front-door.

I went down to open it, and Gregson burst past me into the hallway. He stood at the foot of the stairs, I suspect unsure whether to go up, but Holmes came straight down. I saw he had not rested for he was wearing the same clothes as he had the previous evening.

"I have a new message," gasped Gregson. "We intercepted a diplomatic bag on its way to the German Embassy in Carlton Gardens.

I had no means of transport from Gower Street where my office is, so I ran all the way from there. Here it is."

He handed Holmes a piece of paper and, looking over his shoulder, I could see the following:

"311, 697, 164, 197"

"We let the original go on," added Gregson, still out of breath, "but we took this transcript."

Holmes, Gregson, and I went into my study, and Holmes sat at my desk hunched over the latest message.

"None of the same character-sets as in the first message," I heard him mutter, "but the same number of sets. So still only four of them."

"Could it be a kiss?" asked Gregson.

Gregson saw my blank expression and explained. "A kiss, a term I learnt from Mr Holmes's monograph, is a re-encrypted message – so a message is written in one code and then re-translated into another, as I referred to last night. I only suggest it because, as Mr Holmes says, both messages are the same length."

"I cannot exclude that possibility," said Holmes, "but that merely multiplies our problems as, if what you suggest is true, it means that the Germans have not one but two previously unknown codes in this same three character-set format which contain what must be significant information, and which we have no idea of how to solve. Gregson, I fear I cannot make bricks without straw. I cannot work on this code or codes without more material."

Holmes continued to sit at my desk after Gregson had gone. Eventually he asked me for a piece of paper and wrote a note in longhand which he slipped into his pocket before he spoke to me again.

"I shall have to go to see the Prime Minister, good Watson. What say you to an early morning trip to Downing Street?"

We got the first underground train of the morning and were in Westminster soon after six o'clock. I wonder how many people there might be for whom the Prime Minister might rise at that hour, but Mr Asquith saw us soon after we arrived.

"What can I do for you, Mr Holmes?" he asked.

Holmes told the prime minister about the latest coded message, and then continued. "We are faced, Prime Minister, with at least one new German code and a precarious international situation. One way to break a code, is to create an event which the enemy refers to in a coded message. Knowing what the Germans might be writing about, may make it easier to crack the code that it is in – rather as Gregson was able to crack a code by deducing that the message was about the birthday of the Kaiser. Equally the bombardment of a harbour-town is likely to result in a coded message about that town, and identification of the town in the message will greatly facilitate the code-makers job in breaking the rest of the code."

"What you propose makes sense," responded Asquith cautiously, "but could you be more specific. I cannot authorise the bombardment of German territory just because of the events in Sarajevo yesterday and the discovery of messages in a previously unknown code."

"Under my *nom de guerre*, Altamont, I am held in some esteem in German circles. Why do we not plant a story in the press about the success that British Intelligence has had in rounding up British traitors. It could hint that my position is in danger, and that might provoke the Germans into writing a coded message with my name in it. Altamont lends itself well to such a ruse, as it uses the letter "A" twice and the letter "T" twice and it should be easy to spot the replacement character-set used in a substitution code."

"How would you like this hint to be planted?"

"I took the liberty of drafting an article, which could appear in one of the national newspapers under the by-line 'From a Special Correspondent.'"

Holmes handed the Prime Minister the note he had drafted at my desk and I repeat it below.

"As a measure of the trust placed in this newspaper by the government, our Special Correspondent has been exclusively briefed by sources close to the Prime Minister, Mr Asquith. The government, according to this source, will be placing additional emphasis on rounding up the members of the spy network of the Central Powers based in this country. The source said, 'These people pose a profound menace to our country's interests. We have already arrested two called James and Hollis, and they have been given the treatment reserved for traitors. But we are after much bigger fish. We are aware that disaffected Irishmen in the United States have been a fecund source of traitors for the Central powers. We will root them out one by one and when we capture them, they can expect the same treatment.'"

"To ensure that this article generates a message by the Germans," said Holmes, "it would be as well if it appeared in a newspaper that is only published in London. The press," he added, "is useful when you know how to use it."

"Thank you, Mr Holmes. I shall make sure this story is published by the end of the week."

"And, Prime Minister, I would ask you to use your network of spies in Germany to watch German troop movements carefully. Knowing where such movements are taking place may also be of assistance in cracking this code."

"Your point is clear Mr Holmes, but do not underestimate the difficulties of observing troop movements in a territory the size of the German Empire with borders adjoining Russia, the Austro-Hungarian Empire, Switzerland, the Low Countries, Denmark, and France."

The article Holmes had drafted was in *The London Evening Standard* on Tuesday the 30th of June. As the first edition of that organ is published at eleven o'clock in the morning, I was not surprised when I received a telegram from Holmes that afternoon with the message "Gregson wants to see me again. Will be with you at six."

Holmes was at my door at slightly before the appointed hour and, insofar as he is ever forthcoming on anything, he looked confident of success. "In code-breaking circles, what we have done is known as fishing," he said. "The article is the bait and the Germans seem to have risen to it."

"What makes you so sure that they have responded to the article."

"Let us wait and see what Gregson brings us – although I cannot believe he would have asked to meet me here, if another message in this new code had not been sent – and the timing, straight after my article appeared in the *Evening Standard*, is very promising."

At six Gregson was with us, and he came straight to the point.

"We intercepted this message on its way from the German Embassy at Carlton Terrace to Count von Bork in Harwich."

"My handler," Holmes reminded us with a note of triumph in his voice. "This may be easier than we hoped for."

Gregson handed Holmes a piece of paper and I set out below what the three of us saw that evening:

"316, 497, 313, 327, 839, 723, 839, 753, 583, 193, 88X"

Holmes drew out the two other messages and put them on the table in front of him. He bent himself over the three messages, and his brow furrowed in concentration. My heart sank into my boots at the doleful look on his face when he eventually looked up.

"I fear that even with this additional message I cannot advance."

He pointed at the new message and at the two ones seen previously which I set out below:

"952, 395, 239, 523"

"311, 697, 164, 197"

"The new message contains only eleven character-sets. It repeats only one set within the message and does not repeat any of the other eight character-sets from the other two messages."

"What about the X at the end of the message?" asked a downcast Gregson. "That is something we have not seen before."

"I cannot," replied Holmes thoughtfully, "account for it. It may be a normal part of the code – a total of nineteen character-sets two of which repeat still do not furnish us with much material – or it may be that a modified character-set refers to a specific place, person, or thing of special significance. But, until we find out what that place, person, or thing is, that only makes the matter harder."

Holmes paused and lit his pipe.

"Do not, good Gregson, rest in your search for more messages of this type. They cannot but be hugely important but how I cannot say."

Gregson left, and Holmes carried on staring at the same three pieces of paper.

"Consider this, good Watson," he said at last, "the Germans are only using this new code very exceptionally. My handler is von Bork. And the Germans regard my activities as of supreme importance. You have to ask yourself what else the embassy in London might be writing to von Bork about. And yet they confine the message to eleven character-sets."

"What if we work on the assumption that one of the character sets refers to you under your alias?"

"That is of course a possible hypothesis. But let us say that they wish to say something like 'Altamont in danger' which would be 'Altamont in Gefahr' in German. The remaining character sets would provide ten letters, and within these and the eight character-sets from the other two messages, you would think we would have more than one letter repeated within the message or from one of the other messages. You try to construct a meaningful text with eighteen letters only one of which repeats. It is an impossible task."

"Could more of the character-sets represent words?"

"What you suggest would explain the mysteries of these short texts but would also multiply our problems as we would be faced with a character-set for most words. Basic Japanese has pictograms reflecting whole words. It requires the reader to know a minimum of two-thousand pictograms. You may imagine the difficulties of decrypting a code that has a character-sets that represent whole words in any significant number."

He tamped down the tobacco in his pipe before continuing.

"And you should also consider the impracticality of devising a code with thousands of character-sets that is only used in the rarest of cases. It is hard for the sender of the message to encode and hard for the recipient of the message to decrypt. We must hope for more instances of this code being used."

"I am at a loss."

"So, I fear, am I."

And there the matter rested.

July rolled on. The weather was beautiful, and the events got ever more menacing. By 1 August Germany had declared war on Russia and, on that day, I was called to Downing Street. Sitting alongside the Prime Minister was the foreign secretary, Mr Edward Grey, who gave us a brief summary of events and plans.

"With the Germans and the Russians at war, it is hard to see how we and the French can stay out of it. The lights are going out all over Europe. I do not know that we will see them relit in our lifetimes. Almost every country in Europe is mobilising its troops as each plans how to launch invasions, thwart invasions, or to defend its neutrality."

It was Gregson who spoke next.

"We have intercepted another message in the new code. This is the first for over a month. The German Second Army is based in Jülich, a garrison town thirty miles west of Cologne and its general is called von Bülow. To the north of him is General von Kluck with the German First Army. We have assumed that, as in the Franco-Prussian war of 1870, any German invasion of France would come from somewhere on the line between the Luxembourg border and the sea."

"That is a very long front," observed Holmes drily.

"And I fear," said the Prime Minister, "the message which Gregson has intercepted, only makes the matter more difficult."

"Indeed so, gentlemen." He pulled out of his pocket the three previous messages and the new one which he laid next to each other. "This new message," he added, "was sent from the German chancellor, Theodor von Bethmann-Hollweg, to General von Bülow."

Holmes sat with the messages for some time, but when he raised his head, he looked no happier than he had when he had looked at the previous three messages. I set out the new message and the other three below:

"641, 697, 972, 359, 938, 331, 331, 688, 262, 383, 318, 397"

"952, 395, 239, 523"

"311, 697, 164, 197"

"316, 497, 313, 327, 839, 723, 839, 753, 583, 193, 88X"

"I note," said Holmes at last, "that we have another duplication of a character-set within one message. This new message makes successive use of the set 331."

"That is so," said Gregson. "Yet if the sets refer to letters, then there are only two repetitions in thirty-one character-sets. On the other hand, if the characters in the code are functioning as pictograms, we have no idea what places, people or things they refer to. And a solution where the character sets represent words makes even less sense when one of the only two sets that is produced more than once repeats itself consecutively."

We sat in silence for some minutes before Gregson asked that a map of Western Europe be brought before us.

"I thought I remembered," said he, "a town's name that repeats the same word. Look down here – on the map is a German town called Baden-Baden. Could the repeated 331s refer to that?"

"Baden-Baden," said Holmes, pointing at the map with the stem of his pipe, "is a spa town in the Black Forest. As you can see, it is well to the southeast of the French-Belgian border and then where the Luxembourg-French border meets the German-French border. You can imagine the sophistication of this code if the Germans have made the number 331 represent the word Baden."

"And that is miles from where the French have disposed their main forces," exclaimed Grey. "Baden-Baden is twenty-five miles east of Strasbourg, and the French have no significant forces in the area to meet a major advance from there."

We sat in silent thought.

"And yet I cannot believe that a message in this new and rarely used code is about anything other than troop dispositions," said Asquith at last. He paused before continuing. "But all our intelligence," he added at last, "tells us that the Germans, if they advance, will do so from well to the north as the southern part of the French German border down to Switzerland is heavily fortified and the Massif Centrale behind it is terrain that is hard for troops to advance in. Could this be a feint from the south to get us to move troops down there? Or an encircling movement from the south to link up with troops who advance from the north."

Holmes shrugged, "I cannot advise you on this matter, Prime Minister. You must make the decision on whether to say anything to the French. It would be a grave decision indeed to move forces away from northern France based on a highly speculative reading of two character-sets of a code we have thus far had no success at all in breaking. And the more people you tell about these messages, the greater the chances of the Germans finding out about our ability to intercept their most secret messages even though we have not broken their code."

The meeting broke up shortly afterwards but not before Asquith had made the following statement which he was to repeat at a speech at the Guildhall in November of 1914. "We will not unsheathe the sword lightly. But if we do so, we shall not lay it down until France is adequately secured against the menace of aggression, until the rights of the smaller nationalities of Europe are placed upon an unassailable foundation, and until the military domination of Prussia is wholly and finally destroyed."

As we left, I could see Asquith and Grey utterly bowed by the responsibility with which they were faced.

Holmes again came to stay the night. I knew better than to press a confidence, but it was Holmes who initiated the exchange that followed.

"'Pon my word, Watson. It is good to have you before me. I have had to work solo for two years, adopt the beard that you see, and put on an accent the like of which you will never have heard."

"Perhaps you might elaborate as far as you are able."

"I first attracted attention in Chicago, graduated in an Irish secret society at Buffalo, gave serious trouble to the constabulary at Skibbareen, and so eventually caught the eye of a subordinate agent of the head of espionage at the German embassy, Count von Bork. Since then I have been honoured by his confidence, which has not prevented most of his plans going subtly wrong, and five of his best agents being in prison. I watched them, Watson, and I picked them as they ripened."

"You have, I am sure, done the country great service."

"There is more to come -which is why I am unable to dedicate the time I would like to this code."

"I would be happy to help you in any way that I can."

Holmes sat in silence. He had emptied and recharged his pipe before he spoke again in a hushed tone.

"I have a mission tomorrow. My master provides me with a driver to whom I am most forthcoming about what I claim to do. Perhaps, given the number of my master's spies who have already landed in prison, it would not create suspicion if the one he provides me with were arrested, and I hired one of my own. In this hour of our country's need, good Watson, I would rather have you at my side than anyone else."

My regular readers will recognise what happened next, but I summarise what happened for those who do not.

I drove Holmes, disguised as the reprobate agent, Altamont, to von Bork's house on the coast of the German Ocean (or the North Sea as we are gradually coming to call it). It would have excited too much comment had I, a stranger to the German spy-master, come into the house, but Holmes soon came down to the car to say that he had chloroformed von Bork, and to ask if I would like to join him for a glass of wine.

We sat sipping some quite exceptional imperial Tokay while von Bork lay tied up beside us.

Holmes told me how he had taunted his handler about the arrest of German spies and how von Bork had shown him his safe with the password August1914.

"It is full of documents revealing who the traitors are in our ranks, good Watson. It is the result of three years' work."

I looked around the great hall of von Bork's stately home. "It is certainly a splendid house," I commented.

"It reminds me rather of Baskerville Hall. Particularly this lofty chamber. You remember the paintings of Baskerville's ancestors. Henry Baskerville felt that they were watching him. is of the German nobility, and he has pictures of his ancestors here which he was going to pack up tomorrow to take with him. You can see the likeness of these figures of the past to our prisoner," Holmes waved in the direction of von Bork, "in spite of all the trappings of wigs, hats, and beards…"

Holmes's voice broke off.

"Of course, the trappings…" he gasped.

"What do you mean?" I asked.

"I have the appearance of the messages before my eyes, Watson, but I do not have them with me. I never carry anything with me when on mission for von Bork which could betray what I really am."

"But what has their appearance to do with it? The coded messages were all in transcript."

"Let us waste not an instant in taking the comatose von Bork to Scotland Yard where he can be locked away, and then go to see Gregson."

My readers who know *His Last Bow* may have been surprised at the jocular tone Holmes adopted on that car journey from Harwich to London. As stated previously, this implausible section was inserted at the request of the British government – "If the public is enjoying your banter," said Mr Asquith, "they will not think about what else might have been going on."

In fact, we drove at a break-neck speed to London with Holmes alternating between urging me to drive faster and lamenting, "How could I be so blind, how could I be so blind?"

Once von Bork was safely in the care of His Majesty's constabulary, Holmes and I dashed round to Gregson's office in Gower Street. "Even though it is late on a Sunday," said Holmes, "I am sure that Gregson will be at his desk."

My friend's sense was as unerring as ever. Apart from the security guards, Gregson was the only person in the building. He sat in an office lined with maps, dictionaries in different languages, and books on mathematical theory. He visibly brightened when he saw us.

"We have another message, Mr Holmes. Here it is:

'265, 388, 392, 353, 889, 753, 311, 697, 164, 197, 163, 383, 166, 464, 392, 353, 888, 316, 646, 483, 166, 464'

It was sent late yesterday from Berlin to General von Bülow at Jülich which suggests that he is the key figure in any invasion plans the Germans may have."

"Give me the other messages," said Holmes.

"Here they are:

'952, 395, 239, 523'

'311, 697, 164, 197'

'316, 497, 313, 327, 839, 723, 839, 753, 583, 193, 88X'

'641, 697, 972, 359, 938, 331, 331, 688, 262, 383, 318, 397'

"We could not," said Holmes, "account for why the messages had so few characters and why none of them repeated. But that was only because we were distracted by the commas between the sets of numbers. Let us see what happens if we put the commas between every two numbers rather than every three."

Holmes sat down with a pen and a piece of paper and, after, a few minutes came up with the following:

"95, 23, 95, 23, 95, 23

"31, 16, 97, 16, 41, 97

"31, 64, 97, 31, 33, 27, 83, 97, 23, 83, 97, 53, 58, 31, 93, 88X

"64, 16, 97, 97, 23, 59, 93, 83, 31, 33, 16, 88, 26, 23, 83, 31, 83, 97

"26, 53, 88, 39, 23, 53, 88, 97, 53, 31, 16, 97, 16, 41, 97, 16, 33, 83, 16, 64, 64, 39, 23, 53, 88, 83, 16, 64, 64, 83, 16, 64, 64"

Holmes let his breath out with a hiss.

"Well, at least we can see a pattern now. The third message is indeed about Altamont and we can see that 31 is A and that 97 is T."

"But that means the second message is A_ T_ _ T?" responded Gregson. "I can think of no word that conforms to that pattern in German – and the words in English with a spelling consistent with that are "Artist' and "Aptest" which are clearly irrelevant to our purposes. In French – a language often used in German military circles, I can..."

At that moment the floor to Gregson's office flew open and in strode the Prime Minister.

"The Germans have taken over Luxembourg," he said. "It is good to see you here Mr Holmes and you too Dr Watson. Thank you for your arrest of von Bork, but I assume you are here to crack this code, and this latest turn of events makes the matter imperative."

"I have cracked the letters of the name Altamont, but it will take me time to break the rest."

"We have no time, Mr Holmes. I have told the French about the new code. They were also aware of it, but they too have been unable to crack it. We must know whether the main thrust will come with an encircling movement to link up with the Germans' feint into Luxembourg."

"Encirclement!" exclaimed Holmes. "That's it."

"It's the standard way of launching a mil.."

"Gregson," said Holmes, cutting directly across what the Prime Minister was saying, "Gregson, do any of your books on mathematical theory cover pi – the expression of the relationship between the diameter of a circle and its circumference?"

After some searching, Gregson found an expression of pi to a hundred places.

"Look," cried Holmes! "Pi starts with 3.1 and A is 31. Humans, when they devise numbers for a substitution code, always show a bias towards particular numbers. Using pi as the source of numbers eliminates that."

He went to a desk and drew up the table which I set out below:

A	31	N	83
B	41	O	27
C	59	P	95
D	26	Q	02
E	53	R	88
F	58	S	41
G	97	T	97
H	93	U	16
I	23	V	39
J	84	W	93
K	62	X	75
L	64	Y	10
M	33	Z	58

Holmes shouted in triumph when he had completed the table. "Look!" he cried, "using the numbers of pi as a replacement code for the letters of the alphabet makes G and T the same number - 97. It is not necessarily A_T _ _T. Either of the T's may be – by Jove it is – a G. It is August! The second message says August – the same word as von Bork had as the password to his safe - and the last message says 'Der vierte August um null vier null null' or 'the fourth of August at four a.m'."

"But the fourth message starts with Luttich?" said Gregson, catching swiftly on. "What is Luttich?"

"It is the German for Liège," replied Holmes instantly. "That message can be translated as 'Liège, Namur, Dinant'. Let me summarise all five messages.

'95, 23, 95, 23, 95, 23'

Pi pi pi – as we speculated, this must have been a pre-arranged signal to selected senior German officials that the pi code, as must have been communicated to them previously, was about to be used to carry exceedingly sensitive messages.

'31, 16, 97, 16, 41, 97'

August – this told the senior German officials the month when an attack was likely to take place. It is a weakness of the code that "G" and "T" are the same although this should not be a major obstacle to a code used for the shortest and most secret messages.

'31, 64, 97, 31, 33, 27, 83, 97, 23, 83, 97, 53 ,58, 31, 93, 88X

Altamont in Gefahr – means Altamont in danger."

"Your bait worked, Mr Holmes," interrupted Mr Asquith, "but you had no way of recognising it."

"Another weakness of the code," continued my friend, "is that the number of letters in the message must be divisible by three otherwise the coder has to fill the gap with an invented character. The X at the end of this message was screaming that at me. Fool I was not to realise it although I am flattered that the Germans considered my work so important that they used their special code when they thought I was in peril, and risked its security by making a modification to it which compromised it."

Holmes turned to the last two messages and decrypted:

"'64, 16, 97, 97, 23, 59, 93 ,83, 31, 33, 16, 88, 26, 23, 83, 31, 83, 97'

Lüttich — as I said, the German for Liège, Namur, Dinant — communication of the direction of the planned German advance

'26, 53, 88, 39, 23, 53, 88, 97, 53, 31, 16, 97, 16, 41, 97, 16, 33, 83, 16, 64, 64, 39, 23, 53, 88, 83, 16, 64, 64, 83, 16, 64, 64'

Der vierte August um null vier null null — being the date and time of the first assault — the 4th August at 4 o'clock in the morning."

Holmes turned to Asquith. "The key message is that the Germans will attack Belgium at 4 a.m. on the 4th of August striking at Liège and Namur before swinging south to Dinant. The attack will start in," Holmes glanced at his watch, "twenty-seven hours' time. I would beg you, Prime Minister, to waste not a second in advising our French allies of this plan. I would also plead with you to give the Germans no reason to think that their code has been decrypted. Who knows what they might use it for next?"

"How do you suggest I do that? If our troops are moved to meet this attack, they will know the code has been tracked."

"Could a plane not be used? A plane could fly up over German territory and see the German armies poised to strike across the Belgian border. If one were seen by the Germans and their attack were anticipated, that would give the Germans no reason to think that their code had been broken."

"You seem, Mr Holmes, to be possessed of powers that are barely human."

The Prime Minister was soon on his way, while Holmes and I retired to Queen Square.

We sat smoking cigars and Holmes said, "I fear my temporary deception by the German stratagem of putting commas between every three numbers rather than, as one would expect, between every two, is only explicable by the fact that I was working on a separate case at the same time."

"But you seem to have got everything right," I protested.

"But too slowly. My monograph points out that a delay in decryption is nearly as dangerous as a failure to decrypt. I have failed my own test."

Maybe it was the passing of years, maybe it was a premonition of the slaughter that was to follow, but I have never seen my friend as downcast as he was at this moment which had, uniquely, seen two triumphs for him.

"Perhaps," I asked, hoping to raise his spirits, "you could give your final insights in this case."

"The steps I took to decipher the code – the search for repeated characters, the fishing expedition – were straight out of the code-breaker's text-book."

"Of which the author is one Sherlock Holmes."

A smile came over Holmes's face at this interruption, and he continued.

"But the use of commas to fool the eye into seeing sets with three characters rather than two was an ingenious one. Once the commas were in the right place, the code was fairly easy to crack. You will note all the messages in this code were transmitted on paper rather than being telegraphed, all bar one had a number of letters divisible by three, and the one that did not had a rather clumsy X in it to make it fit the code."

Writing in 1916 and knowing that most of Holmes's war work is embargoed *sine die*, it is hard to know how much of what followed will be at the front of my reader's mind. But, for the record, the Belgians, tipped off by both the French and the British, were waiting for the Germans at Liège and Namur. They conducted a most gallant defence of both, and this delayed the Germans getting through to northern France, thereby giving the French time to get their forces into the right places and to build up their own defences. Had the Belgians been routed in the first days of August 1914, it is likely that the Germans would have broken through to Paris by the end of the month.

It is thus not too much to say that the cracking by Sherlock Holmes of what I shall continue to call the pi code, while not preventing the war or ensuring its final victorious outcome, did ensure that an early defeat for the Entente powers (France, Great Britain, and her empire) was averted.

The Sorceress and the Sea-Lord

The 1880s were a time of major financial shocks in the global economy with large swings in exchange rates, interest rates, and terms of trade. As is the way with such things, the wealthy seemed largely unaffected by this instability, while those of us of more modest means – for example, an invalided-out army surgeon with a weak leg and a weaker banking account, as I describe myself in *The Sign of Four* – viewed the uncertainty with dismay.

The Reigate Squires of '87 occurred right in the midst of this economic turmoil and was one of the earliest of the investigations undertaken by my friend, Mr Sherlock Holmes, that I chose to set before the public, although it did not appear in print until as late as 1894. In it I told of a case that chanced to come Holmes's way while he was recuperating from what I then described as his brilliant resolution of the matter involving the Netherlands-Sumatra Company and the now notorious Baron Maupertuis. I also commented at the time that the events of the latter were too fresh in the public's memory to require enumeration and focused instead on the murder that Holmes investigated at Reigate as this had received only local coverage at the time.

Some years have now elapsed since 1887, and this story now sets out the Netherlands-Sumatra Company case. What I relate will come as a surprise to those who may have thought they knew already the facts of my friend's investigation into that company through what they had seen in the press. As my reader will discover, the way the press presented the matter, as well as the way I presented Holmes's disturbed state of mind at the time of *The Reigate Squires*, were at complete variance with the facts – even though what I presented in the Reigate story was a reflection of what I knew when I wrote it.

I am under no illusions that the disjunction between the appearance given at the time and the reality I present now will result in the text that follows being suppressed for many years, but it is as well that a true and fair record is made. This narrative also includes a discovery about my friend, which will, I am sure, be of the greatest interest to his many followers, and which also, in its own way, demonstrates how deceptive appearances can be. The story is presented in the order in which I became aware of events, as I would like to place my readers in my shoes as matters unfolded with the complexity of an operatic plot. Should they at times feel disoriented by this mode of narration, then they will be sharing the confused emotions that I myself felt during 1886 and the first half of 1887.

The fraud case referred to above had its inception just over a year before it came to the public's attention and in a most unexpected way, which at first sight had nothing to do with any financial matter. In the 1890s and the first years of the twentieth century, my friend was often consulted by politicians – even up to the rank of prime minister – but the summons by the First Lord of the Admiralty, Sir Joseph Porter, for Holmes to come to the Admiralty was the first instance of this. To the surprise of both Holmes and me, the invitation stipulated that I too should be in attendance. When we entered his office in Admiralty Arch on an unseasonably warm day in early 1886, we were further surprised to find that he was accompanied not just by a civil servant but by a veritable entourage of followers – sisters, cousins and aunts, we were told – who chimed into our discussions at every moment.

"I reckon them up in dozens," said Sir Joseph with a breezy wave in the direction of his relatives, before he began the exposition of his case, "I am at present the First Lord of the Admiralty. But I am advised by the Prime Minister that I am soon to be made First Lord of the Treasury."

"Is that not rather a major change of tack?" asked my friend.

Sir Joseph Porter was one of the wealthiest politicians in the land. He had started his career as a lawyer but had ended up developing a chain of stationery shops whose outlets are still to be found in every high street and railway station in the country.

"All in a blind trust now," he assured us, "but when I was a lad," he continued, "I served a term as office boy to an attorney's firm. At this, I made such a mark, I was soon promoted to be a junior clerk. And so, by degrees, I rose to the firm's partnership. And that, Mr Holmes, was the closest I ever got to a ship before I rose to my current position."

Sir Joseph paused to smile at his own joke, and his sisters, cousins and aunts burst into peals of laughter.

"By contrast," he continued, "being First Lord of the Treasury is much closer to the desk-based roles I occupied before I rose to my current office. But it is really all a question of management – whether of ships and fleets, or of interest rates and spending. And in any case, one should not overestimate the influence that politicians can have either on our mariners or on the economy. Admiral Nelson said, 'I cannot command wind or weather.' And so it is for me. As first sea-lord, I cannot ensure that our sailors always enjoy a calm sea and a prosperous voyage and, as First Lord to the Treasury, I will not by any means be able to ensure that our economy always runs on an even keel."

"You make yourself very plain," said my friend, intrigued, I think, as was I, at where this introduction was leading.

"Before I leave my current office," continued Porter, "I would like to do something for which I will be remembered. It has struck me that giving our brave tars improved information on the weather would be of the greatest benefit to them. The better they are informed of the vicissitudes of the weather, the safer will be their passage to defend our great empire's interests. To that end, I would like to commission you to become the Admiralty's first official weather forecaster."

I am not sure what my friend thought he had been summoned to the Admiralty for, but I am sure that being given a commission to forecast the weather had not featured among the list of possibilities. He sat in silence for several seconds.

"I have always considered," he opined at last, "that the weather is largely something that takes its own course. Consequently, attempts to forecast it are based on quackery rather than science."

"That, my dear Mr Holmes," replied Sir Joseph smoothly, "runs quite contrary to what your friend Dr Watson quotes you as saying in his recent work about your activities, A Study in Scarlet. Indeed, it was a reading of your friend's book that caused me to invite you here." Somewhat to my embarrassment, Sir Joseph picked up from his desk my newly published novel, and quoted from it a section he had underlined in red. "'From a drop of water, a logician could infer the possibility of an Atlantic or a Niagara without having seen or heard of one or the other. So, all life is a great chain, the nature of which is known whenever we are shown a single link of it.'"

There was a pause as Sir Joseph held up the book opened on the relevant page. He then continued, addressing Holmes. "Your own words, Mr Holmes, quoted by your friend here, and presented under a heading that you yourself bestowed, *The Book of Life*. And what is more, your friend's work then demonstrates your ability to live up to them. Surely you would not wish to resile from so sweeping a statement just as your reputation as one of the great thinkers of the age is so in the ascendant."

Porter looked at me, I think in the hope that I might support him in his petition. My friend was and remains susceptible on the side of flattery, but it was nevertheless quite a minute while Holmes considered.

"I play the game for its own sake," he said, at length, "and have no desire to move my focus away from criminal investigation. Furthermore, whoever provides the Admiralty with information, will need to be as adept at providing it on Pondicherry as on Portsmouth and I do not have the means to do that for you."

Sir Joseph looked crestfallen at Holmes's remark, but my friend continued. "There is, however, surely no reason why you should not run a competition between interested and reputable parties as to who is best at forecasting the weather. I would be happy to provide you with assistance in establishing such a contest."

"And how might we judge between them?" asked Porter.

Holmes thought for a while.

"You require a means of adjudication that is easy to establish, transparent in its results, and impossible to manipulate. Why not ask them to forecast the next day's London Docks noon temperature and compare their forecasts to the actual temperature as reported in *The Times* for that day? That is simple, not susceptible to contrivance—"

"And most admirable," broke in Sir Joseph, his visage visibly brightening. "We shall do exactly as you suggest." He paused, as though another thought had occurred to him. "We could, if you wish, call the weather forecast the Holmes Forecast as that would provide its users assurance of its reliability, as well as giving publicity to your intellectual services."

Again, my friend looked disconcerted by the first sea-lord's suggestion. Seeing his uncertainty, Porter soothed, "Well, if you do not wish for that, we will perhaps say that the weather forecast comes from the Home Office, even though it would be of most use to the Admiralty. You and I, Mr Holmes, would know the reason why the forecast would bear that name, although we would have to turn a Nelsonian eye to the slight mismatch in what I propose. And the choice of name would not signify anything to anyone else."

And that was the end of the consultation.

I knew that Holmes was further involved in the matter over the next few weeks, but I confess that in the whirlwind of cases in which I joined Holmes's investigations, the peculiar petition I refer to above rapidly slipped my mind. Holmes commented drily to me that the forecasters' main technique seemed to be to assume that the next day's weather would be the same as that of the current day, but I did note with amusement the additional coverage provided by newspapers to weather reporting and to weather forecasting, and how they acknowledged the Home Office as the source of their information.

A year later, the events described in *The Reigate Squires* opened with me travelling to Lyon to tend to my friend whose health had given out following the Netherland-Sumatra case referred to above.

I had been aware of my friend's involvement with a French case as I sometimes picked the mail up on the mat when on the way up from the entrance hall at Baker Street to our flat. Holmes received letters from every country on earth, but the number of missives from France had seen a notable increase. Most came in envelopes with the Baker Street address typed on, while a few – generally letters in small envelopes – came with hand-written addresses. And there was a regular stream of mail which came in bulky white envelopes with the address written in the same hand. These latter epistles stood out to me as, uniquely, the addressor of the envelope applied a downward sloping or *grave* accent to Holmes's surname thus rendering it Holm**è**s (bold font for the **è in** the word Holm**è**s mine).

I picked one of these missives off the mat one morning as I was returning from a trip to the tobacconist's and, when I did so, I was startled to note that one of these envelopes addressed to Sherlock Holmès bore a faint but distinct scent of jasmine. 1887 was still early in my friendship with Sherlock Holmes and, had he moved out of Baker Street, it would have meant that I too would have had to vacate the quarters I had come to regard as home, for paying the full rent of the rooms at 221 b would have been too heavy a burden for my pocket on its own. My reader may therefore imagine that I came to regard these missives addressed to Sherlock Holm**è**s (emphasis mine) with some trepidation, although I knew not what matter my friend was investigating. This concern was exacerbated by Holmes's reaction to them, for, rather than going through them, as he did with the rest of his correspondence, by the fireside in our little sitting room, he retreated with them to his own room. As the early months of 1887 passed, Holmes spent less and less time in Baker Street and more and more time in France – this I knew because it became one of my tasks at this time to redirect his mail to a variety of hotels in Paris and Lyon. And so it went on for several weeks.

It was on the unexpectedly cold 14th of April 1887 that I received the telegram which informed me that Holmes was ill and delusional in his room at the Hotel Dulong in Lyon. Within twenty-four hours I was there. Here he sat, cross-legged and bolt upright in his dressing-gown at the far end of the bed, wracked with the blackest depression. He was unable to focus his eyes on me, and I am not sure that, at my first entry to the room, he even recognised me.

My reader will have noted from previous cases that my main form of medical treatment is to administer a dash of brandy to my patient. In this case, however, I felt a more robust medical intervention was required. Accordingly, rather than ordering a mere glass of brandy, I ordered a large tumbler of the spirit for him, not stinting at its cost in spite of the eye-watering price that a recent devaluation of the pound had imposed. Holmes drained the tumbler in one draught, and it soon brought some colour back to his blanched face, although he continued to sit cross-legged on his bed, maintaining his stony silence.

"I have spent the last two months in a fever of labour," he whispered from time to time in a voice that never seemed to be addressed to me. "I never worked less than fifteen hours a day and more than once kept at the task for five days at a stretch."

"Time for you to come back to Baker Street with me, my friend," I said, and started to put his very limited personal effects into his suitcase.

I wrote at the beginning of *The Reigate Squires* that when I entered Holmes's room, I had to wade through congratulatory telegrams to get to his bedside. I was unsure what to do with these sheaves of paper but decided in the end that I should make some effort to preserve these paeons to his triumph – as the press described the resolution of the Netherlands-Sumatra case – particularly as Baker Street too was full of messages of congratulation. Without paying attention to any one item, I started to add these to the contents of his case. Holmes, for his part, continued to sit upright in bed, his gaze distracted, and so distanced from his normal persona that he did not even smoke.

I got at length to the telegrams lying under the bedside table and was about to start picking them up when a scream issued from Holmes. He mustered his last reserves of strength to leap from his station and seize one telegram which, in the blur as he thrust it deep into the pocket of his dressing gown, I saw was addressed to Mr Sherlock Holmès. When he resumed his position at the end of the bed, it was to shiver uncontrollably.

I felt there was no point in intruding into a matter that was obviously important to him and continued to clear the room. We left a chilly Lyon on the same day. My more attentive readers will have wondered at the timing of our return to Baker Street, which I commented at the time took three days, and now is the time to reveal why it took me twenty-four hours to get to Lyon and three times as long for the two of us to make the journey back.

Although the clearance of Holmes's room at his hotel referred to above was a contributory factor, the main reason for the delay was an incident in Paris on which I have never previously remarked.

As one might expect, the train from Lyon to Paris arrives at the Gare de Lyon in the south-east of the city. During the five-hour train journey, Holmes did nothing other than stare vacantly out of the window and addressed no word to me. On arrival, I hailed the Parisian equivalent of a hansom cab to traverse the centre of the city to Paris Gare du Nord to catch the boat-train to London.

We were rattling through the centre of Paris in good time for the next boat-train, when Holmes, who had maintained his silence, leant forward, and said something to the cabbie. Suddenly our cab struck out westwards and soon, to my astonishment, we found ourselves outside the Paris National Opera House. Holmes descended without a word, and, after using some halting French to ask the cabbie to wait, I got out of the cab to follow him.

I had no idea what Holmes wanted at the Paris Opera at a time such as this, and any lengthy tarrying here would mean we would miss our connection and be forced to make an overnight stay in Paris. I stepped out of the cab into a cold night and, when I caught up with him, I saw he was staring at the posters of forthcoming productions. There was *Don Giovanni* by Mozart, *Fidelio* by Beethoven, and *Samson and Delilah* by Camille Saint-Saëns, a composer whose music I had got to know through Holmes. But the poster on which Holmes seemed to be focusing his attention bore the legend "Annulé" or "cancelled" marked across it. The cancelled production was of a work, *La Montagne Noire* or *The Black Mountain*, and its creator one Hermann Zenta. Both work and composer were unknown to me and the original advertising made much of the fact that the performance of the now cancelled work was to have been its première.

Having looked at the posters, Holmes seemed to have no desire to linger further at the theatre. Without a word to me or even a glance in my direction, he turned and made for the cab. I followed and called out, "Gare du Nord – le plus vite possible" to the cabbie but, hard though he drove the horses, we missed our train to Calais and had to find what was, at such short notice and with the depressed exchange rate, some rather costly overnight accommodation in Paris before we got back to Baker Street late the following evening.

Even back in his familiar surroundings, Holmes's company was most disconcerting.

At this stage of our friendship Holmes still regularly injected himself with cocaine. I have commented elsewhere that his regular dosage was three syringes a day. On his return, this frequency increased greatly so that his arm, which he bared to me at each new injection, soon looked like a battlefield with its mottling of scabs, scars, and puncture wounds. When not exhilarated by cocaine, he would sit staring out of the window smoking cigarette after cigarette.

Rather than the mellow Virginia tobacco he was wont to smoke, Holmes's extended sojourn in France had given him a taste for that country's own style of cigarettes with their bitter-smelling black tobacco, and these altered the ambience of the little Baker Street sitting room even though they offered no attraction to me. Sometimes he would talk to me or – more correctly – at me. The subjects made no sense either individually or taken as a whole – probability theory, barometric readings, and brotherly love were amongst the topics – and I did not attempt to respond. Sometimes he would sing a strain of a melody that I did not recognise, to which he would append words in what I knew to be French but from which I could obtain no meaning. He would then break out into hysterical laughter.

It was at this point that my old friend, Colonel Hayter, tendered another invitation to me to visit. He had come under my professional care in Afghanistan and had taken a house near Reigate in Surrey. He had asked me to come down to him upon a visit on previous occasions and I chanced to go to my club – if the truth be told, to give myself a break from ministering to Holmes – at the same time as the colonel was there. He remarked that if Holmes would only come with me, he would be glad to extend his hospitality to him also.

I felt a change from the centre of London would do my friend some good, but I was unsure how much I should tell Hayter about Holmes's volatile condition. It so happened, however, that when I returned to Baker Street from my club, it was to find Holmes in much the best frame of mind he had been in since his return from France. Once he understood that the colonel's establishment was a bachelor one, and that he would be allowed the fullest freedom, he fell in with my plans. For my part, I confined myself to warning the colonel that Holmes had been suffering from nervous exhaustion.

While we were at Colonel Hayter's house, Holmes conformed to a pattern of behaviour that gave no cause for alarm – no trace of his verbal outbursts or drug addiction – and, like the colonel and me, he confined himself to smoking no more than a modest thirty or so cigarettes a day. The colonel, it emerged, also had a weakness for

French cigarettes, and the two of them placed a special order for them at a local tobacconist. Holmes also pulled off the coup that was his resolution of the Reigate Squires mystery. I thought our troubles were behind us when Holmes said on the conclusion of the case, "Watson, I think our quiet rest in the country has been a distinct success, and I shall certainly return much invigorated to Baker Street tomorrow."

Soon after Holmes had said this, Hayter and I met with the groom to discuss arrangements to get to Reigate Station the next day. When we returned to the lounge, it was to find Holmes unconscious on the couch with a needle in his arm. Whether he had taken a more concentrated cocaine solution than the 7% which was his normal preference, or whether he had overreached his body's capacities with a larger injection than normal, I had no way of telling, but he was comatose.

"What has been happening under my roof?" exclaimed the colonel.

But I was too busy tending to my friend. Although Holmes's unconscious state made the administration of brandy impossible, I did my best to rouse him by pounding at his ribs and shouting in his ear. To no avail.

In the end, a doctor from the local hospital was summoned and, just as my brother-physic crossed the threshold, Holmes, very sheepishly, sat up.

"I fear," he said unsteadily, "as the good Dr Watson has always warned that I might, I have over-taxed my physique."

He passed out again almost immediately before making a steadier recovery about an hour later.

Dr Glitheroe was insistent that Holmes be examined at the local hospital, and my friend was conveyed thither in a carriage. There he was examined by the famous psychiatrist, Henry Maudsley.

"What do you think it is, Dr Watson?" Maudsley asked me.

"A collapse brought on by overwork," I replied cautiously.

"I fear I cannot help you if you will not be straightforward with me," he retorted, and raised Holmes's pock-marked arm. "Have you, as a medical man, not sought to prevent him resorting to these hallucinogenic drugs to which he has so evidently become addicted?"

This was the first of a series of questions which became more and more a reproach to my skills as a physician – indeed they often sounded like the sort of comments I had made previously when trying unsuccessfully to dissuade Holmes from pumping himself full of cocaine. It was not long before I was told that Holmes would be detained in a secure hospital and that I would not be allowed access to him.

It was with a heavy heart I returned to Baker Street. Difficult as Holmes sometimes made the business of sharing our lodgings, not sharing our lodgings for an undefined period was much harder. It was two days later that Hayter came to see me.

"You look washed out, Watson," said he. "Living with your friend can hardly be a picnic if he is an addict of the needle. Why don't you join me on a trip to Paris? If I am not fighting for queen and country somewhere, I often go to Paris in the springtime."

I could think of no more attractive alternative, and the following Thursday saw Hayter and me sitting on the boat-train as it drew out of a chilly Victoria.

"'By the old Moulmein Pagodo, lookin' lazy at the sea, there's a Burma girl a-settin', and I know she thinks of me,'" murmured Hayter an hour and a half later as we caught our first glimpse of the azure of the English Channel from the train. "That's a line I quote every time I head abroad," he said, a light coming into his eyes. "I miss the heat and the excitement of the East when I am in Reigate," he added, as we crossed to Calais on what was an unexpectedly warm afternoon, and there was a pause as he mopped his brow in the heat, before he continued, "but Paris is the next best thing."

Apart from my recent journey through Paris on the way to and from Lyon, I had never visited the French capital, but Colonel Hayter had found us comfortable accommodation in the city centre at a price rendered surprisingly reasonable by a sudden strengthening of the pound. I was exhausted after my recent travails and retired to my room early after a quiet supper.

I was fast asleep when there was a tap on the door.

I padded across the room and opened. Outside my room were two gendarmes. "Est-ce que vous êtes Doctor John Watson?" I was asked.

After confirming my identity, I was told that Colonel Hayter had been involved in a brawl at the Folies Bergère. Between awkward transmission of data in French and English, I was told that the colonel had given my name, and the police wanted me to go along to the station to confirm his identity.

When I got to the police station, my friend was far from his normally chipper self – he had a split lip, a black eye, and burst knuckles on his right hand.

"A pretty mess I have made of things!" he lamented. "I saw a rather attractive lady at the Folies who had, I thought, surrendered her amateur status. I assumed our dialogue would then follow a fairly predictable course, but mademoiselle turned out to have a husband, and he took a rather dim view of my proposition. One thing led to another, and I was as you see me now when the gendarmes arrived."

"So, what is to happen next?" I asked.

An English-speaking officer was present – *agent* Gilbert, he told me his name was – and he said, "It is already after midnight, so we are into Friday morning."

"A tough night for you," I said, trying to be ingratiating.

The policeman smiled wearily. "*En fait,*" he said at length, "the lot of a policeman is a far from happy one on a night like this. Your friend will have to be detained until Monday when we can get him into court for causing an affray. You may visit him tomorrow and Sunday at six o'clock for half an hour, but otherwise you may have no contact."

My reader may imagine my feelings. My closest friend was incarcerated in an asylum and my oldest friend was in gaol. So here I was, in the most beautiful city in the world, with not a soul to spend my time with, and no desire to stay. And yet I felt that I had to stand by Colonel Hayter. Accordingly, I decided I would remain at least until the Monday in the hope that Hayter would be released with a fine. To fill my time, I bought a tourist guide and went to the sites – the Louvre, Versailles, and Notre Dame. I also looked in the newspaper for events that might keep me entertained, and I noted that on the Sunday lunchtime there was a concert at the Paris Conservatoire.

It was not due to start until one o'clock but, to make sure I arrived in plenty of time, I got to the large park in which the Conservatoire stands at well before the appointed time. The building was not yet open, and the park was deserted. It started to drizzle, and I sought shelter on a bench set in an arbour some way back from the main path.

I confess I felt completely wearied and fell into something between a doze and a reverie. My semi-conscious thoughts flitted through my recollections of my adventures in Afghanistan with Colonel Hayter and the cases I had investigated with Holmes. I would have been happy in the company of either and being deprived of any sort of companionship at all was hard to bear. In this brown study, Sherlock Holmes seemed all but tangible but, when I came to, it was to find that the rain had departed, and the Conservatoire's park was filled with people going to the concert. A smell of black tobacco hung in the air.

The main piece being performed was a quintet for piano and strings by another composer whose music had been introduced to me by Holmes – César Franck. The bearded Belgian gave the audience what I assume was a brief introduction to the piece. My French is limited but I picked up "mon quintette dedié à mon bon ami, Camille Saint-Saëns," and noted that he handed the piano score in manuscript form to the equally hirsute Saint-Saëns, when the latter mounted the podium to play the piano part.

It has been said of the English that they do not understand music but that they love the noise it makes. This accords with the way I normally listen – as when I heard Sarasate at St James's Hall with Holmes, or now, as I listened to a new piece by one of Europe's great composers performed by another. I again had the strange feeling that Holmes was present in the auditorium and scanned the audience, as my attention occasionally wandered, but he was nowhere to be seen and I focused back on the music.

The four string players and the pianist were as absorbed in their music as now was I. They were all men, but they were joined on stage by a tall, spare, auburn-haired female who acted as a page-turner for the pianist.

I felt, as I watched, that Saint-Saëns was in some way disconcerted by the music, although I could not put my finger on why I had this feeling. But the accuracy of my instinct was confirmed at the end of the piece. Franck came onto the stage as the audience burst into applause and made to embrace Saint-Saëns. But the latter flung his piano score onto the floor, and then strode brusquely past Franck and into the wings whence no amount of applause would persuade him to return. Somewhat nonplussed, Franck brought the string players to their feet and then, oddly, seized the page-turner round the waist, and advanced with her to the front of the stage to take a bow. I could see that the page-turner was unsure of whether or not to take a bow of her own, but she did so eventually to further rapturous applause.

At length, the clapping came to an end and the audience started to drift out of the auditorium as the quintet was the last piece on the programme. I was probably amongst the last to leave and wandered back out into the conservatoire's garden, which I took the decision to explore as I had nothing else planned until my visit to Colonel Hayter in the evening.

The garden is laid out in a mixture of open lawns and dense clumps of trees with a crisscrossing of gravel-covered and often windy paths. The weather had turned fair with small fluffy clouds dotted across a clear sky and a friendly sun illuminating the trees' fresh blossoms. I strode out, enjoying the mixture of landscapes, for once feeling heartened and not alone, even though my only companion was the comforting cigarette I had just lit.

It was when I turned the corner on one of the paths, which was taking me round a group of dense trees, that I was astonished to be faced by Sherlock Holmes, arm in arm with the striking-looking page-turner from the concert. The lady herself held an infant on the shoulder of her other arm. I would add that my friend, for the sole time in our acquaintance, looked astonished as well, but it was his appearance that shook me. Emaciated and haggard, he was a wreck of the man with whom I shared quarters.

It was the page-turner – the only composed adult out of the three of us – who broke the silence.

"So, my Sherlock," she drawled, although in her heavily accented English, it sounded like "Chère Loque," with a distinct pause between the two syllables, "I observe from the smell of this man's cigarette that he is an *Anglais*, and, from your reaction to seeing him,

I deduce that he must be the Dr Watson with whom it is my fate to compete for your affections."

There was another silence before the angular page-turner, after a glance at my friend, continued.

"Perhaps, *Chère Loque*, you might like to continue your walk with this Dr Watson, for I suspect the two of you have much to discuss."

She turned on her heel and soon disappeared around a corner.

"What is the meaning of this, Holmes?" I exclaimed. "I left London with you confined to an asylum; I come to Paris, and find you arm in arm with a woman unknown."

My friend looked abashed and it was a while before he responded in a quavering voice quite at variance from his normal incisive tones.

"I was able to get myself discharged from the asylum and returned to Baker Street to find you gone. I still felt weak from the ardours of the Maupertuis case and the subsequent excitement at Reigate. I came to Paris where I had some small business to attend to arising out of the Maupertuis case and some ancillary matters that arose at the same time."

"Small business? Ancillary matters? The decision to keep you in confinement was not taken lightly and nor will your discharge have been."

"Perhaps it would help you if I explained fully the matters in which I have been involved," said Holmes, sounding slightly evasive.

"Pray do so," said I, slightly stiffly.

As I have indicated, the events associated with the Maupertuis business were something from which I had been excluded and, as so often with me, finding out what my friend had been doing was of far greater moment to me than any other concerns I might have had. We found a bench, and each of us lit up a pipe. This is my friend's account of events

Earlier this year, I was summoned to the Treasury where I again had an interview with Sir Joseph Porter, who, as he anticipated at our meeting about weather forecasting, had become its first lord.

"We are very concerned by the activities of the Netherlands-Sumatra Company," he began.

This was a name that was new to me and I asked Sir Joseph to elaborate.

"The Netherlands-Sumatra Company is a currency speculator and is quoted on the French stock exchange or the *Bourse* as it is known in French. It takes large positions on foreign currencies which require it to predict the movement of the French Franc against other currencies, but it has a particular predilection for trades involving sterling."

"What is the problem with that?" I asked. "There are lots of companies doing the same thing."

"That is so, but the Netherlands-Sumatra Company takes much larger positions and so takes much larger risks."

Sir Joseph was about to continue when a civil servant burst in. "Sir Joseph," he exclaimed, "the last quarter's economic growth has just been announced and was below half a per cent. It is surely time to lower interest rates to stimulate the economy."

Sir Joseph leant back in his chair and considered. "I feel," he said at last to the mandarin, "the moment is not ripe for such a move. I would not wish that the markets got the impression that each strong quarter of economic growth is followed by an interest rate rise, or that a quarter of weak growth results in a cutting of such rates."

When the civil servant had departed, Sir Joseph turned to me and commented, "Interest rates as an instrument of policy are much over-rated in their effectiveness for steering the economy, irrespective of financial climate. But, to return to the Netherland-Sumatra Company, we would expect it to be hedging its risks with counter-parties which will counter-balance the risks it is taking and yet it does not."

"What, never?" I interjected.

"No never, Mr Holmes. On the contrary, it speculates against future positions in a manner most reckless. And yet its currency bets – for bets is what they are – have a remarkable record of hardly ever being wrong. The Company takes highly risky positions, stakes very large amounts of money on its judgments, and yet its speculations have a remarkable record of success."

"So, what is there for me to investigate?"

"The activities of the Netherlands-Sumatra Company undermine the stability of the currency markets and, as most of their trades involve sterling, we have addressed our concerns to them. This is a matter of particular moment as a French investor, Baron Claude Maupertuis, has made an offer for the shares of the Company at 70% of its current market value on the Bourse. That the shares of the Company should attract so low an offer from him is surprising, and my view is that the speculator thinks he has identified some flaw in the Company's operations. We have agreed with the current management of the Netherlands-Sumatra Company that you will go to Lyon and investigate its affairs."

"But there are firms who specialise in the scrutiny of company accounts who would be far more capable of undertaking such an exercise than I would."

"I fear, Mr Holmes," and at this point the gravest look came over Sir Joseph's face, "that the word of our major auditing firms – Pitt & Waterman, Delatour & Foss, for example – is no longer considered a sufficient guarantor of a company's propriety. It is not long since another major firm of auditors, Trant Gorton, stated publicly that it did not see protecting shareholders from fraud as part of its duties, while the auditors of the building company, Bell & Peal Ltd., were unable to decide whether that company was owed or owed a sum of no less than two million pounds. And yet they still felt sufficiently sure of the probity of the financial statements that they pronounced that they gave a true and fair view of the company."

He paused and I waited to see what he would say next.

"In this matter," he continued eventually, "as with so many others, the word of Mr Sherlock Holmes will carry far more weight with the public than that of any so-called expert, and so set the collective mind at rest."

"And why does the British Treasury need to be involved in this at all? The fate of a French based currency speculator is surely not its concern."

"Ah, Mr Holmes, you underestimate the internationalism of capital markets. Half the British aristocracy has its capital tied up in the Netherlands-Sumatra Company, and its failure would have disastrous consequences for many of the noblest names in the country. And the Netherlands-Sumatra Company's tentacles extend to the City of London as well, so we must consider, based on your work, whether the regulatory control we exercise here is sufficiently rigorous."

"So, what drives currency movements?" I asked.

"The value of a country's currency goes up and down dependent on two main factors. If it is anticipated that there will be a demand for the country's goods which will require purchasers to buy that country's currency, then the country's currency will tend to rise. And if the country's interest rates are more attractive to foreign depositors than that of its neighbours, that will encourage those depositors to buy its currency which will also make its currency increase in value. Equally, if its interest rates are lower or are thought likely to become lower, foreign depositors will sell that country's currency and deposit their money where they can get a higher return."

"You make yourself very plain," I replied. "So, in essence, economic buoyancy should be met by higher interest rates to counter irrational exuberance, while a decline in economic activity should be countered by a lower interest rate to encourage commerce."

I paused for thought as this type of analysis was a new departure for me. Having satisfied myself as to the accuracy of my observation, I appended the remark, "And a change in the interest rate is thus almost an admission that the previous rate was wrong and is hence an indication of a failure in the government's stewardship of the economy."

"My dear Mr Holmes!" exclaimed Sir Joseph. "It has been said that all the economists in the world could be laid end to end without reaching a conclusion. But in spite of your preference for criminal investigation, you have expressed the key facts of macro-economic theory in a few words. Although," he continued, "as with forecasting the weather, moving interest rates is as much a matter of convincing the public that a measure is being taken than that the measure being taken is right. Your pithy summary confirms the wisdom of my decision to appoint you to conduct this investigation."

There were very few further discussions before I found myself on the train to Lyon, location of the marble-columned headquarters of the Netherlands-Sumatra Company, which stands at the confluence of the Rhône and Saôn rivers, next door to the city's ancient amphitheatre. I was soon before its managing director, Monsieur Henri le Piège. The tall Frenchman was effusive in his welcome.

"Ah, Monsieur Holmes," he said, "Bienvenu! We would welcome your seal of approval on our accounts at this time of our travail. We here have nothing to hide but if we did, the world knows that you, if anyone, would find it. You may go where you like within our building, speak to anyone you wish, and look at any document you request."

"And what did you find?" I asked, agog at this further example of my friend's investigative prowess.

"I examined the company's financial records. I examined its correspondence. I looked at the details behind all the accounting entries. I was given full authority to correspond with third parties that traded with the Netherlands-Sumatra Company."

My friend paused, and I was unsure what great discovery he might disclose.

"I found nothing," he eventually said, his eye not meeting mine.

"The company's activities," he continued eventually, "consisted of very few transactions – although big ones. It made its profits entirely as Porter had described to me. That is to say, it invested in currencies that were about to rise, and took short positions on currencies that were about to fall. And extremely good it was at it. I saw from its library of newspapers from around the world that it kept a close watch on the latest developments in the world's economy and was thus well-placed to make the most of speculative opportunities. At the same time, its system of internal control was impeccable, with a clear trail behind every document."

Holmes gave a sigh and inhaled deeply from his pipe at the recollection.

"I tried everything to see a pattern in how they achieved their results: I performed an analytical review of their margins; I went through all their correspondence; I spoke to counter-parties; I had full co-operation from the company's employees."

Holmes pulled again on his pipe and a wan expression crossed his face.

"The hardest thing to deal with," he continued, an unwontedly forlorn tone in his voice, "was my conflict of interest. I found everything in order. Yet my every instinct told me that something was afoot. And all the while I knew that finding nothing was the outcome that satisfied most people – including, uniquely in all my cases, the person who had given me the commission. But no one would make an offer for a company at 30% below its market value without some knowledge that all was not as it seemed. In no investigation I have conducted so far did my work encompass so great a timespan for such meagre findings. I considered drawing up a report which advocated further authorisational controls on process, but, in truth, I had found no official document that had not been counter-signed in triplicate. I reported as much to Sir Joseph when I returned to London."

"And what was his response when you told him this?"

"He told me to take whatever time I needed to get complete assurance on my opinion. Accordingly, I returned to Lyon and spent another two months in a fever of labour. At one point, M. le Piège found me slumped at my writing-desk where I had expired through sheer inanition."

"And what happened next?"

"I telegraphed Sir Joseph in London and told him that I still had no adverse findings on the company's state of affairs. By return I received a telegram summoning me to an urgent meeting at the Treasury." Holmes then continued his narrative.

I was still not sure what reaction to expect from Sir Joseph. Had he wanted me to find some flaw in the activities of the Netherlands-Sumatra Company which, if I understood him correctly, would lead to the ruin of many British families, but which would reinforce his reputation as a politician of sound judgment? Or did he want me to confirm that the current level of regulation of companies was sufficient to protect investors and the market?

My doubts were resolved instantly for Sir Joseph's face broke into smiles when I saw him and expressed my considered opinion.

"This is excellent news," he said. "Your exhaustive researches have revealed nothing untoward. Mr Holmes, if there were an annual prize for auditor of the year, you would not be eligible to win as you would be the competition's judge – and a good judge too. Whatever else may be said about the accounts of the Netherlands-Sumatra Company, they now have received the imprimatur of one of the minds of the age. The trustees of widows and orphans will be able to sleep easy at night. Could you perhaps, Mr Holmes, purely as a matter of form, sign this piece of paper?"

He passed me over a document. It said:

> "I have examined the financial statements of the Netherlands-Sumatra Company. In my opinion, these statements present in all material respects a true and fair view of the financial position of the company."

"But the specialist auditing firms," I objected, "are much more equivocal in what they state about a company's affairs than you are asking me to be here. Indeed, their reports on companies' accounts grow longer each year, and each year the greater length is due to the auditors freighting their reports with more and more limitations on what their own responsibilities are."

"But the specialist auditing firms, Mr Holmes," soothed Sir Joseph, "are not endowed with the preternatural investigative abilities which you possess. They cannot claim as you, with justification, do, to know the whole chain of life from seeing a single link in that chain. Thus, it is hardly likely that they would wish to be unequivocal in their opinions. With your widely discussed forensic skills, I am sure your signature applied to this document will assure the markets that the Netherlands-Sumatra Company is an organisation whose business can be trusted. And the world will be in your debt because you have been able to come to this conclusion."

I signed, and Sir Joseph face became even more wreathed in smiles.

"Your name, Mr Holmes," he purred, "will be in the press this very day."

I was soon on the pavement outside the Treasury. I was puzzled by the extreme pleasure Sir Joseph obviously took in my opinion that there was nothing awry with the Netherlands-Sumatra Company and was sure that I had been given some reason to be so disconcerted. I was still half-lost in thought when I saw on a newsstand across the road the headline, "Sherlock Holmes Signs Off Netherlands-Sumatra Accounts," and realised that Porter had leaked my opinion to the press even before I had signed off on it. As I stood wondering what to do next, the newspaper vendor took delivery of the next edition of the newspaper. This bore the headline, "Major financier arrested".

My curiosity piqued, I crossed the road and purchased a newspaper which contained an article under the by-line of "Our city correspondent".

Holmes reached into his pocket and took out a newspaper cutting from which he read as follows. My older readers will probably recognise the contents of the below from their recollection of the Netherlands-Sumatra case, but I reproduce the full article for those less familiar with the matter.

"There was a bullish mood in the stock markets this morning as Mr Sherlock Holmes, in a fresh demonstration of his investigative skills, confirmed that the recent buoyant results of the Netherlands-Sumatra Company were a true reflection of the company's state of affairs. The surge in the French *Bourse* that Mr Holmes's pronouncement engendered was reflected in gains in the British stock market. The Treasury may need to consider raising interest rates to prevent the economy over-heating.

In an entirely separate development, share speculator Baron Maupertuis, who had been seeking to buy the Lyon-based Netherlands-Sumatra Company at a heavy discount to its market value, was today arrested on tax evasion charges in Paris. As he was led to a secure police carriage, he said to a bemused crowd of by-standers, 'I am guilty of no more than the ability to tell the time.'"

"I remember the turn of events well," I commented, drawing on my pipe. "There was indeed a surge of stock exchange euphoria, not to mention an avalanche of congratulatory mail for you, but you did not return to Baker Street, and the next I saw of you was at the Hotel Dulong. And Maupertuis's remark caused much speculation in London as no one could work out what it meant."

Holmes paused to recharge his own pipe and then continued:

I confess to a measure of anger at the anticipation of my verdict and likewise of curiosity at the arrest of the Baron, and I determined to re-enter the Treasury to make this clear to Sir Joseph.

A security guard made to block my path. "We are under instructions not to re-admit you, Mr Holmes," I heard, but I was able to get past him, and was soon once more before Sir Joseph.

"Why did you anticipate my opinion on the account of the Netherlands-Sumatra Company? And why has Baron Maupertuis been arrested?" I asked.

"My dear Mr Holmes," said he. "I knew that you had no adverse findings from your telegram from Lyon. I wanted to make sure I caught the first edition of the evening newspapers so that your opinion, which you have now confirmed on this piece of paper," he held up the page I had just signed, "was in the news, thus enabling the markets to trade in full confidence of the probity of one of its most dynamic players. And the arrest of Baron Maupertuis is entirely a matter for the French authorities."

"The two matters cannot be unconnected," I objected.

"Mr Holmes, I am not aware there is anything further to discuss. I gave you a task, which you have completed to my complete satisfaction."

"And to that of his sisters, cousins and aunts," interjected a stout lady seated to his left.

"While tax evasion," continued Sir Joseph, "is widely practised in France, and the French authorities are fully entitled to take any action they see fit to combat it. I wish you a good day. The weather is most clement, and I suggest you make the most of it."

Rather than returning to Baker Street, I decided to go back to France to re-examine the records of the Netherlands-Sumatra Company. I was sure that there was some contrivance in its results, which Sir Joseph was at the least aware of, or – more probably – had instigated, and that he wanted me to certify the company's results to prevent any further investigation of it.

By this time it was late and I had to get the night ferry from Dover. On the ship on the way to France, it struck me that any contrivance would require some sort of pre-arranged signal. As I had scrutinized all the company's correspondence, that signal needed to be invisible to any outsider, obvious to any insider, and irregular in its frequency. The next day found me on the train from Paris to Lyon.

We passed through an unseasonal April squall which hurled a flurry of snow and hail against the window of my carriage and the conductor put his head into the compartment to say that our arrival in Lyon would be delayed by ten minutes due to the weather."

Holmes paused, I think expecting an interjection from me, but I was lost for words. He resumed and, as he did so, the tobacco in the bulbous bowl of his pipe glowed red as he approached the moment critique in his chain of reasoning.

"When I got to Lyon, I went to the British Consulate and looked through its archive of British newspapers. What do you think I found?"

"I have no idea," I responded, although I was sure I was missing something obvious.

"Baron Maupertuis had not been referring to the time at all when he said that he was guilty of no more than being able to tell it. In French, the word 'temps' means both time and weather, but the British press had failed to understand what he had said and so had mis-reported it."

I still could not follow the direction of my friend's thought and said as much.

"When I conducted my research at the British Consulate," explained Holmes, in a tone of quite unwonted patience, "I found that each time the day's temperature recorded in *The Times* at London Docks was more than five degrees above what the Home Office had forecast on the previous day, interest rates were raised. And each time it was more than five degrees below what the Home Office had forecast on the previous day, interest rates were lowered."

I still was not sure I had understood Holmes and he explained, "A forecast is published by the Home Office on Monday in respect of Tuesday. If the weather report in respect of Tuesday published in The Times on Wednesday shows a significant deviation from the forecast, interest rates would be raised or lowered. Use of weather patterns to fix interest rates met all the requirements of being clear, irregular, and incapable of manipulation."

"So what was the purpose of the manipulation?" I asked, aghast at the thought that economic management might be being used for anything other than the greater good.

"I will come to the question of motive shortly," replied my friend and resumed his narrative.

My next move on leaving the British Consulate was to head to the office of the Netherlands-Sumatra Company, as I wanted to challenge Monsieur le Piège. I was passing the amphitheatre next to the Company offices, when I saw a large group of ladies forming a queue to visit the site.

I made to hurry on until I noticed in their midst, Sir Joseph, and I realised that he too had been seeking to make his way to the premises of the Netherlands-Sumatra Company, but he had seen me and had sought concealment amongst his sisters, cousins and aunts.

"Did you challenge him?" I asked.

For a second (continued Holmes), Sir Joseph's face froze, and then he said, "I did not know, Mr Holmes, that you too had an interest in Roman history."

"I think your greater interest is in the setting of interest rates to suit your own personal interest," was my riposte.

"Mr Holmes," he replied, "I am here on holiday. I have your written word that the accounts of the Netherland-Sumatra Company are sound, and the only person who might differ in that view is Baron Maupertuis, who faces a long time behind bars for tax evasion – longer if he talks about the affairs of the Netherlands-Sumatra Company. Thus, of the two people in the whole world who have the inclination or the insight to suspect something untoward, one has given his word that nothing is afoot and will not want to rob himself of his reputation for credibility by contradicting himself, and the other is so tainted as a witness that his word will not be believed by anyone."

"But you have acted as a public official to distort the currency markets," I objected. "Pre-knowledge of movement of interest rates through knowing the connection between weather patterns and interest movements is of huge value to currency speculators."

"But I have no interest in doing such a thing. All my assets are held in a blind trust over which I have no control."

"I have no doubt," I countered unabashed, looking at his entourage, "that the blind trust is as blind as Admiral Nelson, whom you are so fond of quoting. And your sisters, cousins and aunts, who seem to accompany you everywhere, will have been aware of the distortion, and will doubtless have benefitted from it by investing in the Netherlands-Sumatra Company."

"Mr Holmes," replied Sir Joseph, "you are accusing me of a crime which has no victims, and you have no evidence of any misdemeanour in respect of a company whose accounts you yourself have certified and have, by doing so, earned great public acclaim. I have acted at all times for the greater good by ensuring the stability of the currency markets. I will now dedicate myself to my interest in Roman history. I would suggest you focus your attention on whatever has brought you to Lyon."

You will not be surprised, Watson, to hear that the office of the Netherlands-Sumatra Company was closed to callers when I eventually arrived there, and I confess that it was the realisation that Sir Joseph had hoodwinked me rather than any great subsequent labour on the case that reduced me to the state you found me in when you came to my room at the Hotel Dulong.

"What are you going to do now?" I asked.

"The Netherlands-Sumatra Company case is at an end. I have stated my opinion on its accounts and have earned thereby the quite unmerited chorus of approval for it to which Sir Joseph referred. The company's inside knowledge on the movement of interest rates will last as long as Sir Joseph is the First Lord of the Treasury, unless, of course, he passes on the secret to his successor.

"But that means Baron Maupertuis will face a lengthy sentence on what I have no doubt are trumped-up charges. Does that not trouble you?"

Holmes would not meet my eye.

"And you have still not disclosed who your lady friend is," I continued. "Or the child," I added, as the enormity of the consequences to me of Holmes having a female companion came back to me with redoubled force.

"The person you describe as my lady-friend, good Watson, is my sister. She has been settled in France for many years and she styles herself Augusta Holmès. It was a condition of my discharge that I have someone to look after me when released and she has been performing that role, which is why I am here."

"And it is she who writes to you as Sherlock Holmès?"

"That is so. I spent my early childhood in France. It was she who conferred on me the pet-name 'Chère Loque', which means "dear wreck" in French, after I had contracted the smallpox as a youth – although her nursing helped me make a complete recovery from the disease. I chose to adopt this pet-name as my official given name when I moved to England, although I anglicised the spelling."

"So, what is your real given name?" I asked, scarce believing that my friend's first name numbered among the misapprehensions under which I had been living.

But Holmes was not to be deflected from talking about his sister. "She has appended a *grave* accent to our family name," he continued as though not having heard my interruption, "and when she writes to me, she adds it to my name as a mark of her affection."

"And she is the mother of that child?"

"She is the mother of no fewer than three children. And," added Holmes, a look of pride ghosting across his visage, "just as I am the world's only consulting detective, she is its only female composer, or *composatrice*. She writes her music under the pseudonym Hermann Zenta to avoid public scrutiny of her activities."

"She composes music?" I asked in astonishment. "Surely, as a woman, she is debarred from studying, and that would make it very hard for her to gain the skills to write music."

"You are right to assume that women are not allowed to study as regular students at the French Conservatoire, but she takes private lessons from both César Franck and Camille Saint-Saëns."

"But even now you have not explained why you have been so occupied for the last weeks and months that you have had a breakdown?"

"Under French law as under English, my sister is a chattel of her husband. He abandoned her and their children, of whom Helyonne, whom you have just seen, is the youngest. Yet, as her husband, he owns the intellectual property of her works, and this means he has the right to receive the royalties on it, which are a substantial sum, as her music grows in popularity. That would leave her penniless. To avoid this, as well as conducting the banking inquiry, I have been feverishly transcribing all her manuscripts into my own hand with a view to claiming in court that her works are in fact from my pen. I carried on this activity out of your sight as I did not wish to explain a private matter, but you have forced my hand."

"What will happen now?"

"Assuming my sleight of hand convinces the French court, I will be able to claim the royalties on her behalf and pass them to her as she tries to make her life as an independent woman."

"Is their transcription such a big task?"

"My sister is to date the creator of three operas, eleven cantatas, many songs, orchestral works, and numerous piano pieces. And she was the author of the words to her vocal pieces as well as the score. So, this was a huge undertaking, especially since I had to make sketches for the works as well as final scores, in order to make my claim to have written them myself plausible in court. I have been copying her life's creative output while dedicating myself to all the other investigations I have been conducting."

My head was spinning at this latest revelation, and I asked, "So what is to happen next?"

135

"The task of transcription is now complete, and the court case to establish my authorship of her works will be heard next week."

"But her husband is a monster. He abandons his wife with three children and still seeks to claim her earnings. Who is he? Is there no law that can touch him?"

Again, my friend paused.

"Her husband is Baron Maupertuis. And he is about to get his just deserts as a gaol sentence will prevent him claiming on his sister's royalties.

"But," I retorted, "the crime for which he is going to gaol is not that of abandoning his wife and family. It is for tax evasion. You may feel he deserves to go to prison for abandoning your sister, but his sentence will be for a different offence. And he will doubtless seek to overturn your claim to have written her works after he is released and, if he succeeds in his action, he will be able to resume his claim on his wife's earnings."

Holmes had no ready answer to my charge of moral hazard and lapsed into silence at this point. But, in fact, Baron Maupertuis got only a light sentence for his tax crimes. Holmes, it turned out, was not the only person to have family in France, and Maupertuis's judge, Serge Siffre-Poitier, Holmes was able to establish, was a second cousin of Sir Joseph Porter.

Nevertheless, arrest and imprisonment dealt a huge shock to the Baron Maupertuis's health, and he went to a little lamented end shortly after his release. This meant that Madame Holmès was able to publish her works under her own name, and Holmes and I went to

Paris to see *La Montaigne Noire* when it received its belated première in 1895. As the first opera by a woman to be staged at the Paris Opera, the piece caused a huge stir in the French press, although the presence of the *grave* accent in the composer's name prevented the British press from linking the work to my friend, so its performance received little coverage in this country.

Finally, my reader may be wondering about the curious end to the concert at the Paris conservatoire, when Camille Saint-Saëns stormed off the stage at the première of Franck's piano quintet.

As might be imagined, after the events described, I took an increased interest in French music – indeed Holmes and I went to the première of the French master's mighty Organ Symphony at St James's Hall in which, as well as conducting his own work, the composer was soloist in a performance of Beethoven's fourth piano concerto under the baton of Sir Arthur Sullivan. After the death of Saint-Saëns in 1921, I read the autobiography of Camille Saint-Saëns, which contained the following passage about Augusta Holmès written in an extravagant style I would not dream of copying.

"This beautiful sorceress was not satisfied merely with cultivating art and preaching art; *au contraire*, she caused it to flourish all about her. Just as Venus fecundated the world when she knotted her tresses, so Augusta Holmès shook over us her reddish locks, and when she was prodigal with the lightning of her eyes and the brilliance of her voice, we creators of art ran to our pens, our brushes, our chisels; and new works of art were born."

The obituary of Saint-Saëns in the *Times* was even more forthcoming. It claimed that both Franck and Saint-Saëns were infatuated by the sister of Sherlock Holmes and that the recently deceased composer had proposed to Mademoiselle Holmès when she was his student (and was turned down by her). It suggested that the reason why Saint-Saëns had stormed out of the concert I had attended at the Paris Conservatoire was that he felt that Franck's work was a musical declaration of love for the auburn page-turner of the manuscript score.

Certainly, the signal of discord between Franck and Saint-Saëns was no less clear than that conveyed by the first sea-lord to the Netherlands-Sumatra Company on the direction of interest rates, and a rather tawdry argument over a woman's affections may well have been the explanation for it.

I would conclude by referring once again to my friend's *Book of Life* article which he penned at the start of our collaboration. Sir Joseph Porter cited it in his commission about the weather and referred to it again when discussing interest rate setting with my friend. After the foregoing, in which macro-economic policy and human relationships had displayed such a disjunction between appearance and reality, it is perhaps unsurprising that Holmes himself never again displayed such certainty.

I should perhaps add that the French courts had no such uncertainty about my friend, Colonel Hayter, who was summarily found guilty of affray the day after the events described above. He was perhaps fortunate that his judge, by coincidence the same Serge Siffre-Poitier who was later to pass sentence on Baron Maupertuis, fixed the fine just after the sudden onset of a hot spell of weather in London had caused a rise in British interest rates.

The resultant surge in the value of the pound meant that the hit to his pocket was considerably less than would otherwise have been the case.

Editorial note by Dr Watson's literary executor, Howard Durham

I discovered Dr Watson's literary *reliquiae* at the Public Record Office in Kew in the summer of 2015 and have been editing them for publication since then.

The identification of a hitherto unknown sister of the great Sherlock Holmes required additional authentication as Augusta Holmès is hardly a household name, but in fact biographical details about her were easily found.

She was born in 1847 and so was, like Mycroft Holmes, seven years older than the great Baker Street detective. The female figure on the cover of this work is she, and there was no shortage of portraits to choose from when preparing this work for publication. Her birth records do not indicate whether she was Mycroft's twin or whether either Mycroft Holmes or Augusta Holmès or both were in fact half-siblings of Sherlock Holmes, or Chère Loque Holmès, as Augusta Holmès seems to have preferred to call him.

I was unable to find any records of a marriage between her and Count Maupertuis, and it may be that the union to which Sherlock Holmes refers was one transacted in secret outside France. French Conservatory records, by contrast, confirm that she studied privately with both Franck and Saint-Saëns, and the latter freely admitted, as the above extract from his autobiography shows, that she was as a muse to him. She was an active composer, and one of the very few French female composers of her generation. Music-loving readers might like to listen to her works, published under the name Hermann Zenta, which are now freely available on modern recordings under her own name. Here is a link to one of her orchestral pieces, *La Nuit et l'Amour*. Readers may also like to listen to Franck's piano quintet which had such an effect on Camille Saint-Saëns. <u>César Franck, Piano Quintet in F minor</u>

Further research also revealed that she did not just serve as a muse to Franck and Saint-Saëns. Even her estranged husband was inspired by her to write poetry under the name Catulle Mendès, and under the link below, readers may like to see a picture by the great August Renoir of Madame Holmès's three children – who are also, of course, the three known nieces of Sherlock Holmes. The original painting is in the Metropolitan Museum of Art in New York. <u>Madame Holmès' Daughters, 1888</u>

Having established that Augusta Holmès was indeed a historical figure as well as the historicity of the events Dr Watson described at the première of Franck's piano quintet, I felt it incumbent upon me to investigate Dr Watson's claim that the British government changed interest rates based on a comparison between the previous day's weather forecast and the actual weather which had been the subject of the forecast rather than in a belief that they had any economic impact.

I confess I considered this suggestion utterly preposterous and assumed that the implausibility of this thesis was the reason for the long suppression of *The Sorceress and the Sea-Lord*.

As the narrative above demonstrates, proving that the British Government sets interest rates dependent on weather patterns is hard to do, but I would point out to the reader the following facts:

❖ WH Smith of the founding family of the stationery chain was first lord of the Treasury from January 1887 to October 1891 – the time frame referred to in the foregoing. Gilbert and Sullivan, in their light opera HMS Pinafore, pilloried him, but referred to him as Sir Joseph Porter to avoid legal complications, although Smith acquired the sobriquet "Pinafore" Smith thereafter. Dr Watson's use of the name Sir Joseph Porter to represent WH Smith was doubtless for the same reasons of legal prudence.

❖ In the four years and ten months that WH Smith was First Lord of the Treasury, interest rates changed thirty-four times, or more often than every other month.

❖ In the hundred-and-six years following his relinquishment of the post they changed on average three times a year.

❖ Since 1997, interest rate setting has been a decision vested in the Bank of England rather than the British government, and over the ten years to the end of 2019, they have changed a mere three times in total.

❖ Over the twenty years since 1999, weather forecasting techniques have so improved that forecasts for four days are now as accurate as weather forecasts for a day ahead were then. This is due to the greater use of satellites and a wider spread of observation posts, enabling developments in the weather to be tracked across a wider area.

It is thus demonstrable that the frequency of changes in interest rates has dropped to the lowest levels ever seen.

Sir Joseph Porter, as I shall continue to call the sea-lord and First Lord of the Treasury, agreed with Sherlock Holmes that a change in interest rates reflected a failure in the government's stewardship of the economy.

It is for the reader to decide whether this greater stability in interest rates is due to improved economic management or to improvements in the ability of meteorologists to forecast the weather.

De Profundis

The horror does not leave me. I have been back in England for many months, yet the matter I am about to relate clings to me still.

I set out the course of events of which I would tell as a story of suspense as this is how I am used to ordering a narrative. Some will feel that such an approach is inappropriate for these gravest matters that I describe. I can accept this criticism but the way I relate events is an accurate reflection of how I experienced what happened. Many of the events of this narrative, no matter when this account is read, will in any case be all too well known to my readers.

Why then, might be asked, in that case relate this matter at all?

I have two answers to this.

The first is that this is a matter of duty to later generations.

Those who witnessed what I was amongst the very first to see must record their memories so that what we saw can never be denied or diminished.

The second is a selfish reason.

I hope that by setting the matter on paper, I can put some distance between it and me so that, while I cannot forget it, it stops dominating my every waking moment as well as my fitful sleep.

My reader will recall that from 1940, Holmes and I lived in a small cottage in Fenny Stratford. Holmes was helping codebreakers at nearby Bletchley Park – something I only became aware of during our interrogation of Rudolph Hess of early May 1945, which I described in *The Führer and his Deputies*. When he was at home, the small garden of our cottage enabled Holmes to continue his chosen retirement activity of beekeeping, while our personal requirements were simple: plain food, tobacco, and newspapers.

While the first Great War had been fought on foreign soil with only limited impact on life within these shores, the second war was felt in every corner of the land whether in the shape of the seemingly unending rationing, the sight of German 'planes overhead, or the presence of families evacuated from London.

Our means of following the progress of events had changed too. In the 1914-1918 war it had been newspapers only, whereas by 1939 we could follow events via the wireless and news reels at the picture house. I would have expected such an increase in the number of sources from which we could obtain information to us might have led to the elimination of false rumours – I had been one of many fooled by the myth of a million Russians landing in Scotland to help the fight at the western front in 1914 – but this did not appear to be the case.

On the contrary there were constant rumours

In late 1939 we heard that the Americans were about to join us in the struggle although their entry to the war had to wait another two years. In the middle of the war we heard of the massacre of thousands of Polish soldiers, which was discovered by the Germans, and which they and the Soviets each claimed was the responsibility of the other. After D-Day, we heard of massacres of civilians in central France, and now at the, end of the war, we heard reports of the British, Americans, and Germans uniting against the Soviets.

With the benefit of hindsight my reader will know that some of these rumours were true, some wholly without foundation, and some a mixture of the two. Holmes kept aloof from all rumours although in hindsight he had access to more confidential information than almost anyone from his work at Bletchley Park and, even at his advanced age, he possessed greater ability than any man alive to investigate matters and to form a picture of what was happening. I did wonder, when rumours circulated of war-crimes, whether my friend would become involved in the investigation of them, but that must wait for another day. It seemed that for now the most heinous crimes had either not happened or had no perpetrator; they were certainly not being investigated.

On Wednesday the 28th of March 1945, there was a knock on the door. I answered it and standing on the step was the spare figure of Field Marshal Bernard Montgomery whose face was well-known to me from newspapers and newsreels. I took him into the cottage's small sitting room where Holmes and I had just concluded a meagre breakfast.

The field marshal came straight to the point.

"Last Friday saw the launch of Operation Plunder. We made landings on the eastern bank of the Rhine at Rees near Cleaves, and our bridgehead, along with that of the American forces at Remagen, is now secure. The war should now end in a matter of weeks."

"That is excellent news," said Holmes, "but what do you want from me? I am ninety-one years old and, although I am in robust health, I cannot see how I might be of help to a field marshal in battle."

"For the further prosecution of the war, we have two contradictory objectives. For political reasons, we want to push our front line as far east as possible in the next few weeks so that as much of Germany as possible finishes the war in the hands of the western allies rather than in the hands of Soviets. But we also want to minimise British casualties. This is desirable in its own right, but doubly important with our troops. Our men are war-weary and see no merit in striving to gain strategic objectives when those objectives will in any case be achieved by our Soviet allies who have no compunction in incurring high casualty rates."

"Pray continue."

"Even though the German situation is hopeless, they continue to mount resistance characterised by skill, bravery, and a complete lack of means. They have no oil-refineries, so their soldiers carry rubber pipes round their necks to recover fuel from shot up vehicles. They have little artillery, so they use hand-fired, single-use devices called Panzerfausts to launch rocket attacks on our tanks. They have little air support and can offer no aerial defence against raids from our bombers and air-attacks from our fighters. Yet they continue to mount assaults on our lines that are measured, effective, and damaging."

"So what is it you wish me to do?"

"You, Mr Holmes, are well-known to the Germans from the writings of Dr Watson here, and his works make clear you have a good command of the German language. We would like you to talk to German prisoners of war that we capture and establish why they carry on fighting even though their situation is hopeless. If we can find out what is causing them to fight, maybe we can find a way of causing them to surrender."

"Have you not already tried to make surrender as attractive as possible to the German?"

"In the fog of war many evil things happen, and surrender is always a huge risk to a soldier who may be shot by his own side or shot out of hand by his captor. But we normally observe the Geneva Convention – as do the Germans – and we do what we can to make sure the Germans we capture are well-treated. We have conducted leaflet drops in which captured German soldiers make this clear, but this has had no effect so far."

Even deep in retirement Holmes was excited by new challenges, and he accepted Montgomery's commission with alacrity. I was asked to provide a record of activities and thus it was that in early April 1945 we were flown from RAF Hendon to Antwerp and then transported eastwards by road into Germany.

The journey was not an easy one. Hitler had issued his so-called Nero command under which everything which might be of use to an advancing army was to be destroyed. Thus, every bridge had been sprung, every road mined, and all open terrain flooded wherever the geography allowed. The town and cities we passed through had been reduced to rubble by our bombers while the villages showed the ravages of the bombardment which had preceded their capture. The roads were clogged with miserable-looking refugees from all parts of Germany. And everywhere hung a stench from the putrefying bodies of combatants and civilians.

We had been assigned to the 11th Armoured Division which had made its field-headquarters in the city of Münster, sixty miles east of the Rhine. Even though the entire terrain between Antwerp and Münster was securely in British hands, it took us nearly three days to traverse the one hundred and eighty miles that lay between the two cities.

We had to approach the city from the south. It had been the subject of a heavy air raid only two weeks before and its western approaches were still impassable. The commanding officer of the 11th Armoured was Major General Philip Roberts, a life-long soldier who had fought in North Africa. We were brought before him and his adjutant, Esmond, on arrival in Münster. He had made his HQ in the city's Rathaus or town-hall, one of whose wings had chanced to remain undamaged.

"It is good to have you here, Mr Holmes," he said, "and you too Dr Watson. We have fought our way up from Juno Beach in Normandy. We have suffered casualties at every turn and continue to incur them. And yet, here we are, well over a hundred miles inside Germany with the Soviets poised outside Berlin. And still the Germans keep fighting even though their cause is obviously lost. The only problem will be the difficulty in supplying you with prisoners. At Normandy, the Germans fought until their position became hopeless, and then surrendered. Here they just fight."

"But do you have prisoners to whom I might speak?"

"I do. We tend to capture the ones who are wounded and can't get back to their lines."

"You mean that they still make incursions in front of their own lines."

"Oh yes. We face frequent counterattacks. They are a constant threat. The Germans are mainly on the defensive, but they are always capable of catching us on the hop with a raid."

"Will the prisoners talk to us?"

"You will see. The town has a palace which used to belong to the local prince. The locals call it the Residenz. We use what has been left unscathed by bombing raids as a hospital and there are about eighty prisoners there. I will call for a truck to take you, and Esmond here will accompany you."

We left Roberts's office and waited for the truck to pick us up.

Holmes was about to strike a match to light his pipe but paused to survey the wilderness of destruction before us. The raids that preceded Münster's capture had been heavy ones and before us was a sea of rubble – just as many British cities had been reduced to mounds of loose brick. He sniffed the air before saying, "I suppose the roads are dangerous; otherwise, we could walk to the hospital ourselves. It's only six hundred yards north west of here."

I was about to ask him how he knew but he turned away from me to shelter his pipe from a small gust of wind.

Esmond drew up in his truck and we headed off. As Holmes had anticipated, the journey we took was a highly circuitous one and Esmond talked to us over the roar of the motor. "We had four prisoners brought in yesterday who were captured making a sortie.

We got them only because the amount of lead we stuck into them meant they couldn't move. I'm hoping they'll all still be alive when we get there."

My time as an army surgeon, albeit over half a century previously, made me able to bear the sight of men with grievous wounds whether they were recovering from them or dying from them, and even to endure the sound of screams from those in pain. But it was the reek of body fluids that smote our senses. With Holmes's command of German and the limited English of the prisoners we saw, communication did not pose a problem and I set out for the record what they said.

The first one we saw was called Kalb. To my horror, he was only sixteen and horribly mutilated.

"I have not long left," he whispered feebly, "but I know that we will have victory and my death will mean that Germany may live. We have weapons in development which you cannot even dream about Mr Holmes. The Vergeltungswaffen - "

"– Vengeance weapons – he means the rocket bombs," explained Holmes -

"Are only a start. Now they devastate London. Soon they will hit New York."

But Kalb's statement seemed to have cost most of the rest of his strength.

His head tipped forward, and bile flecked with clotted blood issued from his mouth. He muttered something incoherent and then started whispering intently what I thought was the Rosary until Holmes translated, "I swear to God this sacred oath. That to the Leader of the German Empire and people, Adolf Hitler, supreme commander of the armed forces I shall render unconditional obedience, and that as a brave soldier I shall at all times be prepared to give my life for this oath."

He started again, his whisper even fainter, "I swear to God", but he broke off to breathe his last with a death rattle that would have shocked in any ambience other than this one.

"Let's try someone else," said Holmes.

Two beds down was a man in his early forties with a broken thigh. His name was Mittler. "We may be beaten but we will never capitulate. Didn't Churchill in 1940 say that the fight would go on even if Britain were occupied. I fought at the end of the last war when we were betrayed by the generals, the politicians, and the Jews. We got a stab in the back from them and signed a treaty that no nation could accept with honour. I don't care about my future or anyone else's. I want to fight to the end even if that means that the Russians and the Americans meet somewhere in the middle of Germany. The fight will go on even if it is confined to terrorist action against occupying forces."

He paused and looked at each of us.

"The Führer talked about werewolf actions. And that is how it will be for years to come. We will make what the Russians did to us behind our lines look like a tea party. The world will never be able to rest easy unless you kill all of us."

Holmes, Esmond, and I were silent, all of us, I think, unsure of how to respond. Mittler broke into song, and Holmes translated, "With German blood in our veins, there is no need to waver, To arms, my people, to arms! We'll no more bow to our enslaver, To arms, my people, to arms!"

The third man we spoke to was called Lemberger. Half his face had been shot off and brain tissue was visible through a hole in his skull. I could tell by his waxy colour he was not long for this world, and bubbles of sweat erupted on his skin at the effort of speaking. "I come from Silesia," he gasped. "I have lost everything. My wife and children were killed in an air-raid. Under the terms of the Yalta Conference, Breslau, where my parents live, will become Polish even though it always been German, just so that Russia can expand its territory westwards. After my family was killed, I never wanted to survive the war." Esmond had to help him take some water before he could continue. "I was wounded at Stalingrad and was on the last plane to make it out. My intent then was to commit a soldier's suicide."

"What is that?" I found myself asking, the horror of what I was hearing having a mesmeric hold over me.

Lemberger peered at me from his one remaining eye

"We come out from cover and shoot at anything we can before we are taken down by the enemy."

Esmond nodded in recognition.

"We have seen quite a lot of that. We kill them when we can get a sufficient weight of fire on them but sometimes, we only disable them. And when an orderly attends to them, they will do everything they can to kill him. One pulled the needle on a grenade as an orderly was trying to get a splint on him. And the German survived for a while even after the grenade had gone off and the orderly was dead. But you can imagine no one wanted to treat…."

"My only ambition," continued Lemberger, cutting across Esmond, "was to take as many of the enemy with me before I was killed myself. My only regret is that I didn't take any more before this happened."

The last soldier we saw was a captain named Ritter. He had lost a leg but was it was obvious that he would survive. He seemed pleased to have someone to talk to.

"I am a professional soldier. My family has been in the Prussian and then in the German army for generations. I've always despised that Austrian corporal. It's almost worth being captured to be able to say that without fear of retribution. This second great war was inevitable after the Treaty of Versailles. As a soldier I do what I am told by the politicians and it didn't really matter after the last war who was in charge. We lost a seventh of our territory after 1918, and our eastern neighbours were all much smaller and weaker than we were. So of-course we were going to try and take back what we had lost as soon as we could."

He stared defiantly at us.

"Where we went wrong was in over-reaching ourselves. We might have got away with getting back the Saarland, uniting with Austria, linking up with East Prussia by eliminating Poland, and taking western Czechoslovakia. Then we were mostly taking back land that had always belonged to us. But Hitler couldn't stop – Yugoslavia,

Greece, North Africa, Russia, and, and, and... Then he declared war on the United States. Sheer madness. Gentlemen, National Socialism was an intrinsically good idea that went too far. And we will lose more territory in the East in the final settlement and who knows what else will happen. It is worth continuing the fight to prevent that."

"But this is Germany's western front and there is no suggestion of Germany losing any territory here. And even with what is proposed Germany will be second only to France in size among Western European nations. Yet you continue the fight," objected Holmes.

"I'm not sure anyone in Germany will believe you about Germany's western borders," replied Ritter with a shrug. "After the last war, the French wanted to expel all the Germans from west of the Rhine and take it for themselves. I am sure they are rubbing their hands together now at the prospect."

"Do you think territorial loss in the west is a real concern among Germans?"

"It is one of many," replied Ritter drily. "But at the moment our soldiers are more worried about being killed, and our women about being raped."

Esmond drove us back to the Rathaus and I subsequently saw Holmes in deep discussion with the divisional radio operator.

It was evening before we were able to debrief Roberts.

"And," asked he, "did you hear anything today that gave you an idea of how to make the Germans ahead of us surrender?"

"I take it you can get the BBC news here?"

"Of-course," said Roberts. "It's five to seven here, and five to six in London."

After a few false starts with the reception, we were able to tune in just as Big Ben chimed.

"This is the six o'clock news on the BBC broadcasting from London," said a familiar voice. After announcing some American breakthroughs to the south of us, the newsreader turned to political developments.

"In a communique issued in Paris today following a meeting between General de Gaulle and General Eisenhower, the French leader expressed renewed disappointment at the proposed border settlement in Europe. 'We want the Germans permanently on the other side of the Rhine. It is hard to motivate our troops unless we can have improved security guarantees on the post-war frontiers.'" General Eisenhower noted the French general's comments. He remarked that if German resistance continued, consideration might have to be given to awarding the whole of the west bank of the Rhine as far as the Dutch border to France in any future settlement to ensure the security of France's eastern border."

The news moved onto other matters, but Roberts looked at Holmes with awe.

"That's a smart piece of work, Mr Holmes. We have struggled to give the Germans a positive reason to surrender in the west, but this might help us."

Holmes shrugged.

"I could think of no other plan. What I have planted will not influence those motivated only by vengeance on others or their own death, but it might make some of the more level-headed members of the Wehrmacht more willing to take the risk of crossing lines to surrender."

Roberts had kindly made provision for us to be quartered in the mayor of Münster's office. I was startled the next morning when Roberts shook us awake. "Mr Holmes, Dr Watson, there has been an astonishing development," he said. "Here in Münster is the mouth of a salient into Germany. Our eastern front line is one hundred miles on from here although there are German forces holding defensive positions much closer to our north and south. We drove the Germans out of Hanover two days ago and they are holding a line in front of Celle, the next major town to the east. At just after midnight last night our wireless operator received a signal asking for a temporary ceasefire."

"Is that a common occurrence?" I asked.

"Ceasefires happen occasionally in close combat – particularly in house to house fighting – to allow for the rescue of the wounded and the clearance of bodies. But this message asked for a ceasefire along a four-mile line. It can only be for something big."

"So why have you woken us?" asked Holmes.

"There is no German speaker in the unit ahead. I need someone I can trust to help with any negotiations. We will be leaving in twenty minutes. I would like you too there, Dr Watson to make a record of events. This may lead to nothing, but it could also be the end of the war in the west."

I will not detain my reader with an account of our journey east towards Celle or how the negotiations to hold a ceasefire were initiated. Suffice to say that two days later Holmes and I found ourselves with Roberts and Esmond a few hundred yards from the front line. Talks had been fixed for the next day. Having come that far, I remember the mood of the soldiers around us as being bright at the prospect that the end was in sight.

Holmes by contrast was at his gloomiest. He stood facing the battle lines with an utterly downcast expression.

"There's an east wind blowing, Watson. I fear the worst."

"When you said that in 1914, it presaged a cataclysmic war, although you foretold that a cleaner brighter England would emerge when the sun came out again."

Holmes ignored my remark and sniffed the breeze, foreboding etched on his features.

Early next day saw us in a tent that had been set up in an open field face to face with a general who introduced himself to us as Weber. We had heard that the German troops facing us were ill-equipped and ill-supplied. Weber seemed to bear this out. The jacket of his uniform looked threadbare and mottled although his cap looked smart enough. I noticed Holmes having a close look at the general's uniform although I could not imagine what inference he might be trying to draw from it.

The notes below are a record of what was said.

"As you no doubt know," said Weber, "we are about six miles west of the Weser river here. We have a prepared defensive line and plentiful supplies. Nevertheless, I would advise you, there is a prison camp two miles behind us. There is a typhus epidemic in the camp and if you attack us it will spread to our men and to yours. Where it might end, I would not hazard to guess but the risk is to be avoided."

"What do you propose?" asked Roberts.

"If you allow us to withdraw in good order across the river, you can have all the land that is still in our hands to the west of it."

"Who will handle the typhus outbreak at the camp?"

"We will leave a group of fifty soldiers behind to keep order in the camp until you take it. They will be under the control of the camp's Kommandant. We would like you to provide us with fifty of your soldiers as a guarantee that you let our soldiers return to our lines once you have secured the twenty-five square miles that we are surrendering to you. When you release these men, we will release yours. What you do after that is up to you."

"How do I know that you have authority to do this?"

"I have a dispatch here signed by Heinrich Himmler, the Reichsführer. He has ordered this wholly exceptional surrender of territory for the reasons I have stated."

Weber handed over a dispatch, and Holmes was able to confirm its contents and its authenticity.

"How long do you need to complete your withdrawal?" asked Roberts.

"We need two days to withdraw to our prepared lines behind the river. When we are complete, we will send up three rockets from the far side of the Weser. We can then meet here, exchange the troops both sides have provided as guarantors of good faith, and make arrangements to resume hostilities."

This was not the discussion Roberts had been expecting and he turned to Holmes.

"What do you think?" he asked in a murmur.

"If typhus becomes an epidemic," said my friend, "it will kill more people than fighting ever will. What is proposed will mean that we come into all the territory west of the Weser without firing a shot. If, on the other hand, we fight and win, we will still have to deal with this prison camp, and it will be much harder to do so if hostilities are still continuing."

"But they will be even harder to engage with, if they are dug in on the other side of a river."

"It is your decision, but a war-time typhus epidemic normally costs three times as many people's lives as combat does."

"He says they are still well-resourced. Do you believe him?"

"Weber is an interesting study. His uniform shows much about where he has been and what he has done. Did you see its markings and its erasu..?"

"Mr Holmes, I need to decide whether to launch an attack and you are focusing on the enemy general's uniform. If the enemy is weak, it is better to launch an attack to rout him here rather than letting him have the chance to regroup on the other side of the river."

"I would, good general, refer you to my previous answers about the wisdom of launching an attack before a camp stricken with typhus."

Again I will not detain my reader with an account of the details of the parleying but a few hours later, having sealed an agreement very much on the term proposed by Weber, Holmes and I were in the front jeep with Roberts and Esmond leading the Division's senior officers driving east from our lines.

My reader will probably know what we found but I will relate events as they happened to us.

One thousand yards behind the lines that had previously been held by the Germans, we came to a sign for a village now synonymous with history's greatest crime against humanity – Belsen. It was about another quarter of a mile after the sign that that the stench hit my nostrils and another quarter of a mile brought us to the source of the stench. There was a barbed wire fence and behind the fence stood thousands upon thousands of people in striped uniforms. As we got closer, we noticed that their bodies were in the last stages of starvation. Depending on when this work is read, my reader may wonder at our surprise as, since the war has ended, the horrors of the giant prison camps built by the Germans have become well-known. But by the April of 1945, there had only been confused rumours from the Soviet front, and no one in the West had known whether to believe them.

We looked for the entrance to the camp which turned out to be on a side-road from the main through-face. All the way round to the entrance, pallid faces stared at us from behind the barbed wire. Yet though they stared, their gaze seemed incurious, as though their senses were so blunted by their condition that they were impervious to stimulation.

At the entrance to the camp was a guard of soldiers in Wehrmacht uniform. One of them saluted us smartly as we approached. He said something I did not understand but which Holmes translated to Roberts and me as an offer to take us to meet the camp's Kommandant.

We drove into the camp and the guard climbed into our Jeep.

If we were in a state of shock from what we had seen from outside the camp, it was as nothing compared to what we felt when we entered. Piles of bodies were stacked high by the side of the road. Walking amongst them were more prisoners whose advance emaciation meant they were scarce distinguishable from the corpses. And the same stench of death and human waste that had assailed our nostrils at the hospital in Münster now almost overwhelmed us.

We soon came to the Kommandant' s office and were ushered inside.

Josef Kramer. He had dark hair, deep set eyes, and the air of a clerk. He was to become known in the British press as the "Beast of Belsen" and was hanged eight months later but, when we entered his office he stood up and saluted. "I am sorry for the disagreeable nature of what you see here, gentlemen," he said. "I can assure you, based on my experiences further east, that things are much worse in camps there."

We learned afterwards that he had previously been at Auschwitz where deaths had run into the millions. We had no way of knowing at this point how many deaths there had already been at Belsen but that was not our priority for now.

Esmond took his pistol out of its holster and was, I am sure, going to shoot Kramer on the spot. Roberts dashed the pistol out of his hand.

"All this, Esmond," he said, "must be done by due process. Kramer," he said, "you are under arrest. We have a job now to save what lives we can here."

"You know perfectly well that you cannot arrest me," replied Kramer calmly, "if you want to do things by due process. I will serve you for two days until you are securely in control of this camp. Then, under the terms of the ceasefire agreement, you must then allow me and the troops under my command to return to German-held territory. Otherwise you will not get back the men you have handed over as guarantors of your good faith."

There was a silence which Kramer himself broke.

"In any case, I was only doing what I was told to do. As the extremities of the German empire have been taken by the enemy, we have had to accommodate more and more prisoners here from other camps. And I have been given no extra resources to deal with them. I have received personal orders from the Reichsführer, Heinrich Himmler, to do what I have done. And what are we going to do now? The camp needs to be run. There are thousands of prisoners."

"Very well," said Roberts, "your men will assist mine in running the camp. I want your men to start digging burial pits. I will arrange for the delivery of food and for the arrival of medical staff."

"You want my men to dig burial pits? But I only have fifty men here. That is a complete waste of resources."

"What do you propose?"

"The prisoners can dig the pits under the supervision of my men. You will not get pits of a sufficient size dug in a short time by any other means."

"You want the prisoners to help dig pits?"

"You have an alternative source of manpower for a task as big as what you have in mind?"

"But the prisoners here are in many cases in the last stages of starvation."

Kramer gave a chilling smile, "They are used to doing what they are told." When he saw the look of horror that came over the faces of Roberts, Esmond, Holmes, and me, he quickly added, "But of course I am only the administrator here. I personally have never killed anybody."

This was too much even for the patient Roberts. He dragged Kramer to the window. Holmes and I followed and Roberts, losing all self-possession shouted, "How many corpses to do you see out there? Do you feel no responsibility for these?"

"I repeat I have never personally killed anyone, and I have had to deal with an unsustainable number of new arrivals following our defeats in the east."

"So, how many prisoners are here?" asked Roberts, I think nonplussed by Kramer's calm.

"It is hard to say. This camp was designed for about ten thousand, but I think there are about sixty thousand here now. Our records have been destroyed so we have no clear idea of how many people we have."

"Sixty thousand people?" gasped Roberts. "But that's the size of a small town."

Kramer smiled nervously. "I repeat, I followed my instructions and I do the best that I can. I was not able to refuse to accept prisoners even though I had no resources to deal with them. If I had refused, I would have ended up a prisoner myself."

In the end matters were concluded very much as suggested by the representative of the enemy and Roberts, followed by Esmond, Holmes, and me, egressed from Kramer's office.

"I must address my officers," Roberts, "before we start our work." Our party numbered twenty who were gathered before the circle of jeeps.

"Men," began Roberts, "I am often asked why we soldier. I say to you now, look around. This is why we soldier. We have a solemn duty to our comrades who have fallen so that we can get this far, and to the people here, who have lost everything, to save as many people as we can."

Under the supervision of British troops, the German guards organized work gangs to bury the dead from among those prisoners strong enough to dig. We tried to help the prisoners with the resources that we had but what our division had for itself was scarcely enough. When Roberts radioed London asking for immediate medical assistance and supplies, he was told that there was nothing available for anything that was not directly related to advancing the war effort.

"What do you think I should do about Kramer?" Roberts asked Holmes. "He has been in charge here for a year and he should be made to face justice. I do not want to hand him back to the Germans even though that was part of the agreement we struck with them. Who knows whether we would get him in front of a court after the war?"

"I have already given the matter some thought. Let us wait until we see the German general again."

"And how can I get the resources I need to deal with the prisoner camp?"

"I am dealing with that matter as well. Let us make do with what we have for now," replied my friend.

Right on schedule a day later, three rockets went up on the other side of the river and Roberts, Esmond, Holmes, and I met the same party of Germans as we had done previously.

Weber started. "We have moved our troops across the river, and we are ready to end the ceasefire as long as you are securely in control of the prison camp."

Roberts replied, "We too are ready to restart the fighting. I have been to the prison camp and seen the conditions there. I want to keep Kramer as a prisoner along with the troops guarding the camp. Kramer is a war criminal."

"You know that you cannot do that," countered Weber. "I do not know anything about the conditions in the camp, but I am sure that Kramer was doing the best he could with what he had available."

"You know nothing about the conditions in the camp?" asked Roberts, eyes wide in disbelief. "It is only two miles behind your front-line, you knew there was a typhus outbreak there, and you were tasked with securing a wholly unprecedented ceasefire as a result of those conditions?"

"As a military man you will know that securing your own front-line is quite enough of a responsibility without worrying about a prison camp. And I have nothing like the resources that you do. I will not renege on a deal and, if you try to do so, there will be nothing similar offered ever again. You might like to think about that as the Russians advance unchecked on our eastern front."

"I find you an interesting case-study, general," broke in Holmes. "The word uniform is something of a misnomer as each soldier's uniform is slightly different depending on where he served. Your uniform is a good example of this."

"I have been where my country has asked me to go, and I have served it to the best of my abilities," said Weber stiffly.

"I note that your general's cap had an interesting insignia last time we." My friend pulled a notebook out of his pocket and started to draw. I was standing next to Holmes and saw him sketch out the following device.

He handed it to Weber with the words. "And I noted your jacket's speckled appearance last time we met which could only mean you had had various devices, badges, and stripes removed from it. But you had failed to pay sufficient attention to your cap which had this device on it which you have wisely seen ft to remove. It was the wolf's hook or the Wolfsangel you had on it last time. It shows me that you are from the 2nd Panzer Division which was responsible for the massacres at Tulle and Oradour-sur-Glan in France. And you are a general, so I know your real name is Lammerding."

Weber flushed angrily. "I do not answer personal questions. I repeat, I do what my political masters order me to do to the best of my ability. I do not query my orders and I do not look to the left nor right to see what else is going on around me. Besides, I only arrived at Tulle after the killings were over."

"We may choose to arrest you here for war-crimes"

"If you do that, you will never get your fifty men back."

"But we will keep Kramer and his crew. And you will face the justice of the French."

There was a long pause and Weber, whom I will now called Lammerding, spoke with all the assurance out of his voice. "You can keep Kramer, though not the others, on condition that at the end of the war, the British give me a guarantee that I will not be released from their custody into the hands of the French. They will want to pass a death sentence on me but, if the British protect me, I can go about my normal life as an engineer once the war ends in a few weeks. And I want the same deal for Felder and Grau here," he added nodding at his translator and adjutant.

I could see that this was something that Roberts was most reluctant to allow. I think that Lammerding also saw that he had to make an additional offer.

"Behind us is the city of Celle. It is a garrison town with the most modern and best protected barracks in Germany. It would be very easy to mount a sturdy defence of it which would cost you many men. But if you give me another two days, I will draw my next defensive line behind Celle so that you can have the city without firing a shot."

"How will be able to justify that to your superiors?" asked Roberts disbelievingly.

"There was a recent escape of prisoners from a train bound for the prison camp. I can tell my superiors that typhus has broken out there and conditions in Germany are too chaotic for anyone to check."

Roberts turned to Holmes.

"What do you think?"

"My dear General Roberts, our prime duty must be to the prisoners at Belsen. Every minute we spend here, more people will die there. I have no love of this dealing, but everything else is secondary to our duty to minimise loss of life at the camp."

"You are right, Mr Holmes. Let us return to our lines."

When we were back at our encampment, Roberts was told that a large contingent of journalists from Fleet Street and the BBC had arrived.

"That's all I need," he said. "How did they find out about what is happening here?"

"I suggest," said Holmes, "that you wait and see what happens once they have filed their reports."

That evening we once again gathered round the wireless and listened to the BBC news from London. The Belsen prison camp, or concentration camp as the BBC journalist put it, was the first item. "British soldiers fighting east of Hanover have made a gruesome discovery. At the village of Belsen is a concentration camp, a prison camp set in fields. Our reporter, Richard Dimbleby has filed this report, 'Here, over an acre of ground lie people dead and dying. You could not see which was which. The living lay with their heads against the corpses and around them moved an awful, ghostly procession of emaciated, aimless people, with nothing to do and with no hope of life, unable to move out of your way, unable to look at the terrible sights around th...."

Roberts leaned over sharply and turned the wireless off. "It is my duty to deal with this," he said. "Mr Dimbleby is a great reporter, but no words can do justice to what we have seen."

Esmond came in. "The wireless operator has told me we will get the medical support and supplies you asked for, sir. We just got the message from London."

Roberts stared at Holmes with a look of disbelief on his face. "You seem, Mr Holmes, to have powers that are scarcely human."

"It is the least that I can do," said Holmes soberly. "I feel I have nothing much more that I can offer you here as, for the moment your task as a soldier must be to organize the saving of lives rather than ending enemy lives. You must arrest Kramer before he is due to be handed back to the Germans although he is only a small cog in a wheel. The gallows await him, but we must get to the people to whom he answered if true justice is to be served."

I will provide my reader with a summary of what happened next at Belsen before moving onto the epilogue of this account.

Kramer was arrested the day after the conversation above and faced the trial followed by the punishment to which I have referred. Amongst inmates of the camp, deaths continued at a shockingly high rate even after it was liberated. Many were beyond the help of medicine and nearly a quarter of the sixty thousand who were alive when we took it, had died within two months. The camp itself was burnt to the ground as the buildings harboured not just typhus but other killer diseases such as cholera and tuberculosis but Holmes and I were back in England when this happened.

It was in mid-May that Holmes and I were summoned back to Germany. The chaos on our return was even more palpable than it had been a month previously. While efforts were being made to clear the piles of rubble, many roads were still mined, buildings booby-trapped, and many areas inaccessible.

And then there was the search for criminals.

Playing cards had been printed out and circulated with pictures of the most wanted men. Hitler was, inevitably, the ace of spades, and the other aces were Göbbels, Himmler, and Göring even though the latter had been captured after the cards had been printed. They stared out at anyone who got a pack – Hitler with his toothbrush moustache; Göbbels with his look of malevolence; Himmler, like a junior clerk with his pencil-like moustache and rimless glasses; and Göring looking gross and thuggish.

The wildest rumours abounded and would continue to do so while these and so many others remained unaccounted for. The death of Hitler had been announced but no body found, and there were suggestions that he had escaped the capture of Berlin. Hitler was variously rumoured to have fled to South America, to be hidden in the Alps, and to be living submerged in a submarine. Göbbels appeared to have disappeared without trace, and there was no knowing where Himmler was.

Lammerding had sought out Roberts's division and had asked for British protection from the French who were already seeking his hand-over. Now Holmes had been detailed to interrogate Lammerding on what he knew of the Tulle and Oradour-sur-Glan massacres to establish what had happened and find out what other people should be sought in connection with the atrocities.

Roberts's men had been amongst the British troops who had made an advance across the south of the Jutland peninsula in early May of 1945 so as to forfend a Russian march for the same territory from the east. The British advance had been swift but costly – Esmond had been killed by a sniper at Roberts' side only four hours before the German surrender was announced.

Roberts greeted us outside his quarters in a schoolhouse at Bremevörde about twenty miles west of Hamburg by a bridge across the river Oste. The crossing was controlled by a guard post.

"I have seen my men die in Tunisia, France, Belgium, and Germany but it is heart-breaking to have lost Esmond so close to the end of the war. Now," he said, "I have to deal with Lammerding. And it will be to enable him to escape justice. Let us bring him before us and see what he knows before I pass him up the line. Still, at least Kramer will face trial on a capital charge."

A stream of miserable looking people in German military uniforms were making their way south across the bridge and they were being checked as they crossed. Roberts looked at them and commented, "I sometimes feel pity for them but when I need to take a more objective view, I look at pictures from Belsen which I keep with me at all times."

Holmes, Roberts, and I stood watching for a few minutes more until something suddenly caught Holmes's attention. "The group of three," he said, pointing at some bedraggled men, one in civilian dress with a patch over his left eye and the other two in military uniform who were approaching the sentry post. "it looks as though the two in military uniform are escorting the man in civilian clothes yet one of the soldiers is a lieutenant colonel and other is a major."

"Do you want me to stop them?" asked Roberts.

"If you would be so kind."

Roberts went to the sentries to organize the detention of the three people that Holmes had noted. "A recently shaved off moustache on that man in civilian dress," murmured Holmes to me, and even my eyes could see that the man's upper lip was a lighter colour than the rest of his grimy face. "And he has marks on the side of the nose."

The man's papers were examined. Roberts came over to us. "The papers are false," he said. "They belong to a sergeant-major called Hitzinger but the stamp on his demobilisation papers was made with a coin."

Burgess a tall, bespectacled sergeant brought the prisoner into Roberts's office.

"So where have you been fighting?" Holmes asked the prisoner.

"I am now in the north, but I was fighting in the west," said our prisoner evasively, his one eye rolling in its socket.

"Now then Hitzinger," said Holmes, "we have your demobilisation papers here, but the date is obscured by dirt. Could you have a look and confirm the dates to us."

The prisoner squinted at the grubby piece of paper.

"Do you need glasses?" asked Holmes solicitously. "Burgess, perhaps you could lend Hitzinger your pair, if his are missing, and see if they help him."

I could see that Burgess's astonishment at this request, but he complied and placed them on the prisoner's head.

Hitzinger was still struggling with reading his papers and Holmes walked over to him and flicked the eye-patch off the prisoner's head.

Suddenly Hitzinger was gone and in his place was the insignificant clerk-like presence of Heinrich Himmler whom we had just seen from the playing-cards.

He looked calmly up at us. "I am rather glad to be revealed in my true form," he said, and Holmes translated. "I am of far senior rank to anyone else left in this country. The Führer is no more, and I was his nominated successor. I insist that I be taken to see Field Marshal Montgomery or General Eisenhower."

"Look at this," snapped Roberts, and showed Himmler some of the pictures he had from Belsen. "And Kramer told us that other places were worse. Eight tonnes of human hair were found at Auschwitz." He looked as though he were about to attack our prisoner but then he mastered himself. "Tell me why I should not just shoot you out of hand?"

"Do you know what it is to disobey a command from the Führer?" asked Himmler plaintively in reply.

"But you are yourself a Führer. Your title was Reichsführer and you had the power to order a ceasefire at Belsen. Did you need instructions from Hitler to do that? The culpability of Kramer and of others will be established by a process of law and I am sure their defence will be that they were only obeying your orders. You have no such defence. You knew what was happening. You could have prevented it happening. I will not be happy till you are dangli.."

There was a crunching of glass and a sudden smell of burnt almonds filled the room. "Fool I am," shouted Holmes, "not to think he might have a capsule of poison in his mouth."

I froze for a second and then remembered my medical skills, I punched our prisoner in the stomach with all the might my frame could muster in order to make him vomit. Orderlies were summoned and emetics were forced down Himmler's throat. But all to no avail. In fifteen minutes, he was gone. As he lay before us, he still had the air of a minor civil servant.

Holmes and I completed the debrief of Lammerding over the next few days and about a week later we were back in Fenny Stratford. It was only then that the reaction to what we had done over the previous month set in. Food was scanty enough anyway in that summer of 1945, but Holmes starved himself, and I was completely unable to leave our cottage. My sight started to fail – a common experience among men subjected to the horrors of Belsen and other camps – although it has now largely returned. And, in my early nineties, I count myself fortunate that I have had so many years behind me with hopes of more to come when such a lifespan has been denied to so many of my fellow men.